THE VENGEANCE YOU CRAVE

MADDISON KINGS UNIVERSITY #4

TRACY LORRAINE

Edited by My Brother's Editor

Proofreading by Sisters Get Lit(erary) Author Services

Photography by Armando Adajar

1

LUCA

Since coming back to Maddison after the holidays, I've been out here in the dark every night.

The fury I felt when I discovered that she'd managed to slip out the back and avoid me still burns through my veins.

I'm still desperate to stand in front of her, to demand that she finally tells me the truth, finally confesses to lying but I've settled for watching her.

I might have only had glimpses of the woman—the girl—I gave my heart to all those years ago, but it's easy to see the differences. Starting with the hair. Peyton always had the lightest, softest, prettiest honey blonde hair.

The pink is cute, sure. She's clearly trying to make some kind of statement with it.

But it's not my Peyton.

And while I might hate her, I also crave that girl with the easy, infectious smile who could make me laugh without even trying and light up my entire day with only that smile.

Reaching up, I run my hand through my hair as I think back to those years, how easy they were.

Sure, I had pressure from Dad pressing down on me even back then. At the time I thought it was awful. I remember demanding that Mom make him take a step back, but what I didn't appreciate was that he was going easy back then. Because the years that followed, right now, is unbearable.

A part of me wishes that I wasn't any good on the field. That the first time Dad threw me a ball, I fumbled, tripped over my own feet and shattered all his dreams. Although, I can't help but wonder that if that was the case then he'd have gone out of his way to 'fix' me.

Dad's game days might have been over, but by the time Lee and I were old enough to catch a ball, he knew his dream was going to continue, just through us.

It's exhausting.

The second he discovered that I was quarterback material, he turned all his focus onto me. He wanted me to be his prodigy. Leon was still very much on his radar, but I was the one he really turned his attention to. Lee has no idea how lucky he was, how lucky he is, not being constantly told that you're not good enough, that you called the wrong play, that you made the wrong decision.

I blow out a long shaky breath, my fingers wrapping around the wheel in front of me until they hurt. I need to feel something other than the anger, the disappointment, the crushing loss of everything that's gone fucking wrong recently.

That's why I need her.

I need something that I can control. I need to feel like I can be the one making the decisions, pulling the strings, causing the pain. Because everyone has taken everything else away from me. The pressure, the failure, the lies, the cheating, the bullshit. All of it needs to end.

A roar of frustration rips up my throat, filling the silence of my car as I try to expel the growing feelings within me. I don't even know what they are. Desperation probably.

I'm drowning. Falling deeper into the darkness, and I have no idea how to claw myself back.

I remain in my car, in the darkest corner of the parking lot like I have for the past week and wait. I thought I wanted to stand before her and demand answers, but watching her and knowing she has no idea settles something inside me.

Maybe if I watch for long enough, I'll discover the truth.

I'll catch her out in a lie.

But I know that's unlikely, we haven't seen each

other in almost five years. I have no idea who the girl I once knew is now. I have no idea why she's even back here.

I've run through all the possibilities in my head. I've searched for her on social media. But I haven't found an account in her name, let alone any answers.

For those, I need her.

My fingers twitch with the thought of reaching out and touching her. My mouth waters for all the ways I want to show her just how much her lies hurt. How badly she broke me back then before Letty turned up like a guardian fucking angel and helped me put the pieces back together.

I thought when Letty arrived at MKU it was for me. I truly fucking did.

But now I know differently.

Because all this time, I've been waiting for *her*, and I had no idea.

The second someone pushes the back door open casting a bright glow across the parking lot, my eyes snap toward it, praying that it's time for her to leave.

When it's not her, but a guy taking some trash out, my teeth grind in frustration.

I need her. I need my fucking fix.

I've never been addicted to anything—okay, maybe the game—but this is different. This incessant need for her, the excitement about seeing her wide, fearful eyes when I finally catch up with her. Fuck. It makes me feel more alive than I have in weeks and I fucking love it.

4

I've lost everything else, but this, this right now, is mine and only mine.

I have the control when I reveal myself. I have the control with what I do and what I say for when that happens. No one can take this away from me.

2

PEYTON

I chew on my nail as I sit in the parking lot watching the other students around me head toward the buildings ready for their first classes of the day. But I'm frozen. My stomach is in a tight knot with fear racing through my veins.

I'm a mess. Everything is a fucking mess and nothing makes sense other than wanting to hide. But that's not who I am. I'm stronger than that. Mom raised me to face my demons and to tackle them head-on, not to run like others... like her.

I lower my hand when I have no nail left to bite. It's a habit I thought I cracked in high school, but with everything that's happened in the past couple of months, they're as red and sore as they've ever been.

However, this could be the worst decision I've ever made in my life.

I know that Aunt Fee is right, that I can't just turn my back on everything I've achieved so far, but starting here, at MKU where I know he is. It already feels like a disaster waiting to happen.

As I stare at the smiling students as they catch up with their friends after the holiday break, the dread only gets heavier in my stomach.

I think back to Christmas Eve at The Locker Room and the look in Luca's eyes when he realized it was me. I expected the shock the first time he laid eyes on me again, but what I had hoped was that he'd have moved past what happened between us before I left Rosewood all those years ago, but the second his shock morphed into anger I knew it was only wishful thinking.

I blow out a long breath, my fingers wrapping around the steering wheel in front of me.

Maddison Kings University is huge. The chances of me bumping into him are slim. That knowledge is one of the reasons why I allowed Aunt Fee to convince me to fill out the transfer papers.

"You can do this," I tell myself. "Mom would want you to do this."

With my head held high, I climb from my car, dragging my purse with me and throw it over my shoulder.

I studied the campus map before leaving the house this morning so I think I know where both of my classes today are.

The huge, imposing Westerfield Building looms before me as students funnel through the huge double doors at the front. All my classes this semester are here. Seeing as I was starting over, I decided to make my life as easy as possible and choose classes in my comfort zone. English.

Reading and writing have been the only things that have allowed me to get out of my head these past few weeks, and without them, I have no idea how I could have come through it all.

As the majority of the students inside head for the elevator, I go for the stairs. I don't have time to work out so I've got to get exercise in, wherever I can. My job requires me to be in top form because my boss is a pig and I can't risk losing it.

He's already taken a risk by allowing me to start working before I turn twenty-one, the last thing I need to do is piss him off by adding an inch to my waist.

I make quick work of the two flights of stairs and I'm soon approaching room 305 for my morning class. I follow the other students inside and find myself a seat about halfway back.

I scan every face as I climb the stairs. I don't know why I bother, I already know he's not here. I'd feel it if he were. Just like I did that night.

I felt his presence as I worked the room, clearing empty glasses and taking orders, but I refused to turn around and discover who was causing that kind of reaction within me. Nothing good could come from someone paying me as much attention as I knew the man behind me in the shadows was.

When Bry, the bartender, passed me over his

order, I almost refused to take it over. But knowing I didn't have a choice if I didn't want to draw attention to myself, I swallowed down my apprehension and turned his way.

I knew that at some point it was likely to happen. I wasn't going to move to his territory and get away without him finding out. But this was the last place I was expecting to discover the ghost from my past.

I applied for the job on a whim, thinking it was probably one of the only places surrounding the university where students might not hang out. How wrong was I because not even a week into my position and there he was. My old best friend, the boy who used to know me better than I knew myself, was sitting there mentally imagining all the ways he could make me leave as fast as I had the last time.

Only, he's going to be disappointed because this time, I'm not going anywhere. I need to be here. I've got people depending on me not to screw this whole thing up.

My life has changed in ways I never could have imagined since Mom packed up mine and my sister's shit and drove us out of Rosewood without looking back.

I understand why she did it. She thought that getting Libby away would help to put her on the right path. She had no idea that the months and years that would follow would only get worse.

I pull my notebook from my purse and rummage

around the mess for a pen as I keep an eye on all the students who continue to stream into the room.

There was a time when I wouldn't have needed to even think about what class he might have taken. I knew everything there was to know about Luca Dunn. I knew his dreams, his fears, I knew exactly what made him tick, until I confessed what I had discovered and I realized that maybe I didn't know everything about him after all. Or more so, that he didn't know me because I thought he knew that I'd never lie to him. That no matter how hard something was to tell him, that I'd always do it if I thought it was the right thing to do. Turns out, that wasn't how it was because instead of accepting what I'd said as the truth, he fed into every one of my insecurities and turned against me.

I wished so hard that what I told him wasn't true. But I knew in my soul that it was and that no matter what his reaction was to it, that it was going to change all of our lives. And I couldn't have been more right because only days later, I returned home from school to find Mom packing up our belongings and the three of us drove out of town, never to return.

To this day, I have no idea if it was the right thing to do, but I understand why she did it.

She wanted to protect us. Our safety was more important to her than anything else.

But a part of me wished she'd handled it differently.

I wished we could have stayed and fought for

what was right, to stop it from happening again. Maybe if we'd have stayed, I wouldn't have been in this position now.

Eventually, the stream of students comes to an end and our professor joins us before setting up his presentation and starting the class.

The second he starts talking, even if it's to lay out what we can expect from the course this semester, I forget about everything that's falling apart around me and focus on him.

This is my safe place, my escape from reality. I soak up every single word he says, and already I can feel the tingle of excitement when he talks about the assignments we're going to be expected to complete. Anything that involves me tapping at my keyboard immediately makes me feel lighter.

Folding up the campus map and sliding it back into my pocket, I walk around the corner of the building. The scent in the air makes my mouth water.

The sight of the beans on the sign hanging above the door makes me smile and without a second thought, I head inside.

Thanks to classes just ending, the line is almost out the door, but I join the line prepared to wait until my next class if it means getting my hands on the biggest cup of coffee this place has to offer.

Much to my relief, the line moves quickly and

before I know it, I've got a cappuccino in one hand and an oatmeal raisin cookie in the other.

I walk through the seating area in the hope someone is about to leave so I can sit. It's not all that cold outside but I'd rather be in here, ideally at the back of the room so I can watch the people coming and going, but there's nothing.

Balancing my cookie on my takeout cup, I pull my purse up higher on my shoulder and take a step to leave. I guess it'll have to be a bench outside after all.

"You can sit here," a soft female voice says from behind me, making me look over my shoulder to see if she's actually talking to me.

Spinning around, I find a petite blonde smiling at me and pointing to an empty chair at her table.

"A-are you sure? I don't want to interrupt."

"Of course not," her friend says, clearing away some of their trash from the other side of the table to give me space.

"Thank you," I say sincerely, looking between the two of them.

"I'm Ella and this is Letty," the blonde says, tilting her head to her dark-haired friend beside her.

"H-hey, I'm Peyton, and this is my first day," I add, in case it's not abundantly clear that I have no clue what I'm doing.

"We guessed," Letty says as I lower my ass to the chair.

"I transferred from Trinity Royal," I explain.

"Ah, South Carolina, right?"

"Yeah." I pull a chunk of my cookie off and throw it into my mouth. Neither of them asks why I've moved here and I don't offer up any information either.

"I only started at the beginning of the year. I was at Columbia before that."

"Oh wow, Columbia."

"Yeah, it was pretty incredible, but things... things didn't work out."

"Life doesn't always turn out as we expect, huh?" I ask, more to myself than anyone else.

"You got that right," Letty mutters, lifting her coffee to take a sip.

"So," Ella asks. "What classes are you taking this semester?"

The three of us fall into easy conversation and before I know it, we're having to clear our table and head to class. Ella and I walk back toward the Westerfield Building while Letty heads elsewhere.

"Where are you living? In dorms or..." Ella asks after a few minutes of comfortable silence as we get ourselves set up for class side by side.

Making friends here wasn't all that high up on my to-do list. Surviving has been my most pressing issue the past few months, but I can't deny that having someone beside me, who I think could potentially become a friend, doesn't feel incredible.

It seems like forever ago that I could let my hair down and have a night with the girls without the stress of real life weighing me down. And although I may have found a couple of possible friends, I still can't see a carefree night out happening any time soon. I've got too many responsibilities now, too many people relying on me.

"I'm actually living with my aunt off campus. Well, she's not actually my aunt but..." I trail off realizing that Ella probably doesn't care about the finer details of my life. Well, not bullshit like that anyway, I'm sure she'd more than happily listen to the dramatics because even after living through it all, I still find it unbelievable as if I'm living out a freaking movie.

"That's good though, it'll save you a ton of money."

"Y-yeah, it will," I agree because she's right, and if it weren't for Aunt Fee, then there's no way I'd be able to be here right now. She really is a guardian angel. I dread to even think what my life might be like right now if she didn't reach out and offer to help me.

"The Kappas are having a toga party Friday night to kick off the new semester. You're in, right?"

"Uh," I hesitate. "Actually, I have to work."

"What?" she says, but I can tell from her face that she understands. "That sucks."

I shrug. "Yeah, but I need the money."

"Fair enough. Where do you work?"

Thankfully, our professor follows a couple of latecomers into the auditorium and immediately demands all of our attention and puts a stop to me having to answer.

I won't lie about my job. I'm a waitress in a bar. I might just skirt around the name of said bar because even from only being here a few weeks, I know that the girls who work at The Locker Room have a certain kind of reputation. To be honest, from the things I've both heard and seen, most of them warrant it. But I'm not like them. Yes, I'm there because the pay is better than any other bar in Maddison County, but I have zero interest in the extracurricular activities that can come with the job. I might want the money, but not that bad.

Much like my morning class, I lose myself in the lecture and everything the professor has to say about the course and I eagerly write down our first assignment, already excited to get some words down onto paper to argue my case about whether fraternities promote misogyny, an interesting topic seeing as I was just invited to a party where we all have to wear nothing but sheets, of which I'm sure would cover up as little skin as possible.

"What classes do you have tomorrow?" Ella asks as we make our way out of the building surrounded by others who are equally excited to get out.

"Um... I've got a morning lecture, then I'll probably spend the rest of the day in the library."

"I'm in all day, but do you want to meet us for lunch? I'm pretty sure Letty is free in the afternoon, maybe she could study with you."

"I don't need babysitting." My voice comes out harsher than I intend and Ella's brows pull together, her shoulders dropping in disappointment.

"No, no. I know. That wasn't—fuck. I'm sorry. It's just... you seem like our kind of girl, you know. I didn't want you to be lonely."

"I know, I'm sorry. I'm just not used to..." I gesture between us. "This."

"I know I can be a little full-on at times. But when you know, you know. You know?" She wiggles her brows in amusement as a small laugh passes her lips.

"Yeah, I know." Although really, the only one I thought I knew that with, turned on me, so maybe I'm clueless. "Lunch tomorrow sounds great."

"Yes," she hisses. "And see if you can get Friday night off. It's gonna be a banging party, and I know a few guys who'll love you."

"Oh, no, no. I'm not—"

"I'm not setting you up, don't worry."

"It's fine. Just... just tell me they're not football players," I beg.

She studies me for a beat, one of her eyebrows lifting in curiosity.

"Some are, yeah. They're good guys though."

I can practically hear her silent question, but I speak before she gets a chance to ask.

"I'll take your word for it. Listen, thank you for today. I really appreciate you taking a chance on me, but I really need to head out."

"Work?"

"Yeah."

We quickly agree on a time to meet tomorrow and after Ella taps her number into my cell and calls herself to get mine, she leads me toward the parking lot.

Feeling much more positive about this fresh start than I did when I pulled up this morning, I head home to grab some food and check-in before heading to work.

I stare at myself in the mirror in the staff bathroom at the bar. I hated the dress code—if it can even be called that—from the moment I first stepped inside the building and saw the girls. I knew what to expect from the internet but still, seeing it in real life was entirely different.

But equally, I knew that if the manager would give me a chance that there was no way I was going to turn it down. People do much worse than show a bit of skin for extra tips. Hell, I could be doing a hell of a lot worse for it. But I draw the line here. The paycheck means I get to do fewer hours and hopefully continue with college.

Win-win—I hope.

But since seeing *him* here that night, I seem to spend all my time looking over my shoulder. He warned me that I wasn't getting away, yet, but by some miracle, I was able to slip out of the back door unnoticed at the end of my shift, which incidentally I spent at the other side of the bar so I didn't have to serve him again.

I lied to Bry, told him that Luca was an ex that I didn't want to be anywhere near, and thankfully, he allowed me to switch with another waitress for the rest of my shift.

Touching up my lip gloss, I tuck the loose strands of hair from my updo behind my ears and square my shoulders.

He's not been here since, much to my amazement. He seemed pretty adamant that night that he'd wanted something from me, but it was also clear from his glazed expression that he was drunk.

I convinced myself more each day when he didn't show his face that it was just the drink talking and that just like the day I confessed what I knew, that he didn't want anything to do with me anymore.

I'd hoped that when the time came, that if he turned his back on me once more that it wouldn't hurt as much as it did the first time. And while our time apart and the distance between us has softened the pain somewhat, knowing that what we once had has well and truly been severed, still sends a searing pain through my chest.

I thought Luca was the one. I truly thought we were going to live out everything we'd planned over the years. We were going to go to college, he was going to go into the NFL, we'd get married, have two kids, two dogs, and live happily ever after. We'd even chosen the style of house we wanted. The only thing we never pinned down was the location. Luca had a few top teams he was desperate to be signed by, but he was sensible enough back then to keep his options open. His dad, however, had other ideas and wanted him to follow in his footsteps and join the Atlanta Falcons. Luca was open to it, but he hadn't put all his eggs in one basket, or he hadn't back then. Everything could have changed now.

But two weeks from that night, and I'm still waiting—hoping—that he might show back up and follow through on his threats. I've lost count of how many times I've planned what I might say to him when we come face to face once more, but now that time is closer than ever, I'm questioning everything.

I want to believe that time's a healer and that we can move past what happened. I'm not stupid, I know we'll never have the kind of relationship we did when we were kids. What he did when he walked away from everything we had is something I'm not sure I'll ever truly forgive him for.

Shoving my purse into my locker, I tuck the key into my bra and head out.

He's not been back—at least not when I've been on shift—since that night, so I have no reason to think that he'll be here tonight.

3

LUCA

I'm sitting at the island in the kitchen when the guys spill through the front door a few hours after our last class of the day.

They all went to a diner for burgers seeing as the season is out and we actually get a bit of free time. Me though? I headed straight for the training facility to put in my second gym session of the day.

"Ah, here he is. Our dedicated QB," Colt barks, eyeballing the remains of my chicken salad that's still on the plate in front of me.

Lifting my hand, I flip him off as he yanks the refrigerator door open and begins tossing bottles of beer at the others who are loitering by the door.

A few look at me with their brows drawn in concern and others with confusion, but none more so than my twin brother.

"You coming to hang or continue being a boring

fucker?" Colt continues, ignoring the death stare I'm shooting his way.

"I'm busy, asshole," I mutter, casting a glance down at the textbook in front of me.

"Alright, fuck, Luc." He holds his hands up in defense as he and the others disappear in favor of the den.

"Taking this semester seriously, huh?" Leon asks, closing the door and cutting off the noise from the others.

"Something like that," I mutter.

Things are still strained between us since I discovered that he's been lying to me for years about sleeping with Letty.

I know I should probably just let it go, but I can't. I didn't think Lee and I had secrets. Hell, I didn't think Letty and I did, not back then anyway. I know we kinda went our separate ways a little after high school when she left for Columbia, but still. To know that they'd been together and I had no clue.

Fuck.

I scrub my hand down my face, my anger with both of them threatening to explode once more.

If I discovered this at any other time, I'm sure I'd have just dealt with it, but it's just another thing on top of a whole pile of shit I don't know how to work through.

I hoped that getting back here and taking it out in the gym would have helped, but while that takes some of the need to fight out of my body, my head is an entirely different beast and that wants to hurt anyone who comes close.

"Did you need something or are you just loitering to piss me off?"

"Mom's worried."

"Right?" I ask. This isn't news. She either calls or messages me daily after I skipped out early on the holidays, preferring to be back here and stalking The Locker Room for sights of Peyton.

She probably has every right to be worried, but like fuck am I confessing to that.

"Luc, I wish you'd just—"

"Just what? Forgive you for fucking my best friend and lying to me about it for years?"

"We never lied to you," he says with a sigh.

I get it, I'm fed up with having this same argument too but no matter what, I can't get past it.

"No? So how come I didn't have a fucking clue about it until that cunt told me?" That's the bit that really stings, that I had to find out from someone I can't stand. Someone who now claims to love Letty more than life itself. Fuck, he even fucking proposed.

My teeth grind and my fist curls around the pen in my hand as I think about that image of her with her black diamond engagement ring on her finger.

A fucking black diamond. What fucked up kind of asshole buys a girl a black fucking diamond.

"We were in the wrong, okay. We should have told you. We know this. We've both told you this. But it's in the past. She's not even yours."

The memory of what happened in my bedroom with the three of us last year slams into me. I can still smell the scent of her perfume and remember just how soft her skin was. I can also vividly remember exactly how my brother looked with his head between her thighs.

Letty was mine. At least, that's what I thought.

Turns out that I never really stood a chance.

They always say the bad boys always win, and I guess Letty and Kane are just proof of that.

She loves him for some fucking reason I've yet to see after the way he's treated her. I just really fucking hope that he doesn't screw it up and hurt her even more. Despite being pissed at her, she doesn't deserve to have her heart ripped to pieces.

"You need to talk to her," Lee says, being able to read exactly who I'm thinking about.

"And you need to leave me the fuck alone."

His eyes hold mine as he lifts his hand to push his hair out of his eyes. The anger and frustration, along with a hint of disappointment, reminds me so much of our father that it actually makes my chest hurt.

Even miles away, that controlling fuck manages to get into my head.

"Luc—"

Standing so fast, the stool I was sitting on crashes to the floor, I stand nose to nose with him.

We're the same height, the same build and I know we're matched in the strength department, so when we go at it, we can both hold our own.

My chest heaves in anger that he has the audacity to stand there and tell me to just put everything behind me.

My fists clench and unclench as my heaving breaths wash over his face.

"Go on, asshole. Hit me if it'll make you feel better."

My jaw pops with my restraint.

I know that for a few seconds after the pain shoots up my arm that it will be really fucking worth it, but having to look at his fucking bruised, smug face afterward, no fucking thank you.

"You need to get out of my face," I warn, my voice low and rough.

"I wasn't the one who put myself here, bro," he quips with a smirk that I really want to wipe clean off.

Lifting my hands, I slam them down on his chest, forcing him to back up.

"You need to focus on your own bullshit life, Lee, and keep your fucking nose out of mine."

He throws his head back and laughs.

"Yeah, because it's that fucking easy when I'm watching you self-destruct, bro. We didn't make playoffs, so what? You're still one of the best QBs in the country. You didn't get the girl. Yeah, well, I think we both know that you were always better off as friends anyway. Letty was never it for you. I 'lied' to you. I'm fucking sorry, okay. But you can hardly stand there and tell me that you've never lied to me."

My lips twist in frustration as I take another step toward him.

"Like... where have you been sneaking off to every night since I got back here, huh? Who are you fucking?"

All the air rushes out of my lungs knowing that I've been caught.

"I'm not fucking anyone," I scoff.

"Yeah, I know because you're acting like a whiny little bitch who needs to get laid."

"Fuck me, Lee. Tell me how you really feel," I mutter.

"Will it make a difference?" he asks, his eyes wide. When I don't respond, he takes it as my answer. "You need to sort your shit out. No fucking team will want you next year if you're acting like a fucking pussy."

Snatching up my shit from the counter, I abandon my half-eaten dinner and blow out of the room, more than fed up with Leon's opinions about my life.

The guys are all shooting the shit in the den when I pass them on my way to the stairs. They hear me coming and their voices drop for a beat but when they realize that I'm not joining them, they soon start up again.

Taking three stairs at a time, I finally hit the top floor and lock myself in my room.

It should be a new year, a new semester, and a fresh start, but I can't seem to drag my ass out of last year.

Pulling my cell from my pocket so I can put some music on in the hope of drowning out my misery, I find a stream of messages from Dad.

"Fuuuck," I roar, throwing the thing across the room until it collides with the wall with a satisfying bang.

Stumbling back, I crash into the door and slide down until my ass hits the floor.

Tipping my head back, I suck in some deep breaths.

Leon's right. I know he is. But that knowledge pisses me off as much as all the other shit.

As kids, I was always the one who appeared to have my shit together while he was the loose cannon with his emotions but as the years have passed, we seem to have switched roles and I fucking hate it.

He manages to keep a lid on everything and moves through each day smoothly, where I feel like I'm wading through quicksand, sinking faster than anything else.

"Oh look, it's booty call time again," a voice says from the darkness behind me.

"You a fucking stalker?" I shoot over my shoulder.

"No, but you could well be. That or you're about to rob a bank," he says, appearing from the kitchen and walking around me, taking in what I'm wearing.

"What I'm doing has fuck all to do with you, bro."

"I'll remind you of that when I'm bailing you out of whatever shit you're getting yourself into."

Shaking my head at him, I march toward the front door without so much as a glance at him.

Where I'm going is the only place that makes sense right now. Seeing her is the only thing that makes everything fade into nothingness. The anger of my life dies out and gets replaced with something even more toxic.

My need for her.

As I have been every night, I'm in the space at the very back of the almost empty lot. Hidden under the low-hanging tree which scrapes across the roof of my Audi when I park.

I turn all the lights off and slide down in my seat as I begin my wait for her to slip out the back.

Thanks to Leon's interruption, I'm later than I have been the past few nights, and she doesn't make me wait long.

My heart jumps, my pulse thundering so hard I can feel it in every part of my body as the light from inside the building fills the other end of the lot as she emerges and, with her head down, heading for her own car.

My fingers curl around the wheel with my need to get out and see her, but once I do that, all of this is over.

She's wearing an oversized hoodie. A man's, probably. A boyfriend's? That thought makes bile rush up my throat.

The thought of someone else having her makes me feel murderous.

She was always so pure, so innocent. There's not a second of our time together that I've forgotten before she ruined everything with her lies.

But all that's gone now, hasn't it? She's working in Dad's seedy, exclusive sports bar, shaking her ass for any asshole who wants to look at it.

What happened to her?

The Peyton I knew would never have done that. She was desperate to hide in the shadows and it took all of my persuasive skills to get her to dance with me at school dances. She preferred to just let me get molested by the cheerleaders than to be up there and being judged by them.

I never cared though. I loved that she wasn't one of them, that she cared more about a person than their appearances or the hobbies or sports they played. Same with Letty.

I know for a fact that if Peyton never said what she did, if her mom didn't drag her away then I never would have touched a cheer slut, or a jersey chaser.

She was it for me. Even at fourteen, I knew that. Hell, I'd known a lot earlier than that, I just didn't understand it then.

Reaching down, I palm my dick as I think about everything we shared together. The firsts we gave each other.

Fuck. What I wouldn't give to get a little bit of that right now.

But who else has had a piece of my sweet girl since then?

The second she starts her car and pulls out of the lot, I turn my lights on and follow her out.

To this point, I've only followed her to the end of the street and allowed her to turn left while I've gone right and back to the house.

But tonight is different.

Tonight, I need more.

So when she turns left like usual, so do I.

I hang back, but not too much. Quite honestly, if she wants to pull over and confront me, I'm all for it. Not that I think she'd have the balls. I'd fucking love it if she did though.

The thought of looking into her scared silver eyes again gets my dick hard every single time.

I follow her through town until she turns up a street lined with houses that I really wasn't expecting.

She pulls to a stop alongside the sidewalk of an old bungalow. The building itself looks dated but really well-loved, with lights illuminating the porch and flowers that cover the deck out front.

I park on the other side of the street a few cars down and kill my lights.

There are two other cars parked in the driveway and all the lights are on. Whoever lives here are either night owls, or they're waiting for her.

My heart thunders in my chest as I think about the possibility of the owner of that hoodie waiting to welcome her home from work with open arms.

My hands wring the steering wheel as she throws her door open and heads for the house.

She's not even halfway up the driveway when the front door opens and a man emerges. It's too dark to make out much about him, but Peyton's excitement is obvious as she takes off running and jumps into his arms.

My stomach churns, bile rushes up my throat to the point I think I'm going to have to open the door to puke.

They hold each other for a few seconds and thankfully, my stomach settles and I'm not forced to look away from them.

He takes her purse from her and leads her up to the front door, closing it behind them and cutting off my view of them.

"Motherfucker." I slam my palm down on the wheel time and time again in my need to expel my pent-up aggression. But right now, nothing short of marching up to that door and letting it out on whoever he is will suffice.

4

PEYTON

I can barely keep my eyes open as I drive home after my shift. Once again, there was no sight of Luca, so I can only assume that he's got better things to do than to come after me for shit that happened between us years ago.

Part of me is glad. My life is hard enough right now, the last thing I want to do is rehash the past and try to plead my innocence and convince him that I only told him what I found out because I thought he deserved to know. But the other part, the part that deep down still misses the boy who stole my heart and touched my soul, craves that connection we once had.

In all our years apart, I've never found anything close to what we had.

He was my best friend. My everything. And I'm pretty sure it would have continued that way. We certainly never did anything wrong, anything to deserve to be ripped apart as we were.

Every muscle in my body aches as I throw the door open and climb out.

All I want to do is curl up in bed, but I know I've got a few hours to go yet. I've got assignments that I need to make a start on. This isn't going to work if I fall behind on day one. And I have to make this work. The future isn't just about me anymore. I have people relying on me to provide a future.

It's not unusual that Aunt Fee is still up and the lights are on, so I don't think anything of it as I walk toward the house. That is until the front door opens and someone steps out.

"Oh my God," I squeal when I register who it is.

My exhaustion is suddenly forgotten as I run into his arms.

"I didn't know you were coming," I say as he returns my embrace, holding me tight.

"I didn't tell anyone. Surprise," he says, releasing me and holding his arms out to the sides.

"Aunt Fee must have lost her shit."

He chuckles at me. "She was pretty excited."

"Man, I wish I was here to see her face."

"Come on," he says, wrapping an arm around my shoulders. "She's made you something to eat."

Guilt floods me, I hate that she feels like she needs to stay up and make sure I'm okay. The deal with moving in here wasn't for her to look after me.

"My boy's home," she announces with a wide smile on her face as we enter the kitchen.

Elijah's a Marine and has been on tour for months after being based on the other side of the country. I know that Aunt Fee is mega proud of him, but she also misses her youngest something awful.

He's the same age as my sister, and although they were always closer growing up, the two of us connected after she left. He was at Trinity Royal, and Mom insisted on cooking him a decent meal once a week and doing his laundry as a favor to Aunt Fee. He obliged because, well, what male college student could turn down the offer of free food and laundry services. But it gave us a chance to chat. He was the only real friend I had after leaving Rosewood, which is kind of embarrassing because he's basically family. But my heart and trust were in tatters post-Luca so it's not all that surprising really that I didn't let anyone in.

Aunt Fee places a bowl of mac and cheese in front of both of us and excuses herself for a few minutes.

"Mom says you're working at a bar," he says, suspicion evident in his tone along with his raised eyebrow. "How'd you swing that?"

"My charm, I guess."

"What bar, Peyton?" he growls, putting on his protective big brother act.

I shake my head at him, really not wanting to get

into it. Elijah grew up in Maddison so I have no doubt he knows all about the things that go on behind closed doors inside The Locker Room. "It—"

Thankfully, Aunt Fee walks back in cutting off whatever I was going to say in the hope of changing the topic of conversation.

"It's so nice having you all here," she says, going to the cake tin on the side and pulling the lid off.

"Is everything okay?" I ask, knowing that she went to the back room.

"Perfect. Nothing to worry about." She smiles at me softly, but although she says the words I want to hear, she knows full well that I'll still worry. "How was work?" she asks, completely ignoring the obvious tension radiating from her son because there's no way she'd miss it, she's too perceptive.

"You know, the usual. Busy."

"Have you cut your hours yet? You know it's going to get too much, now classes have started." She pins me with a look while Elijah's eyes burn into the side of my face.

"N-no, not yet. I want to do as much as I can."

"Pey," she warns.

"I know what I'm doing," I argue. *I have no clue what I'm doing.*

"I trust you, but I'm worried. I know you're strong, but you can't take on the world single-handedly."

I pick at my mac and cheese, still full of the food she packed for me and sent me to work with. When she pulls out her homemade cake, Elijah's eyes light up but I make my excuses and leave them to get caught up.

I quietly poke my head into the back room to make sure everything really is okay before I make my way upstairs to my room.

It's tiny, barely more than a closet, but it's got everything I need and it's a hell of a lot more than I'd be able to afford if I were out on my own right now.

Ripping the hoodie from my body—one of Elijah's I stole years ago when he stayed with us for a week or two—I grab a clean pair of pajamas and head for the shower to wash the scent of the bar off me.

I walk onto campus the next morning already feeling like I belong. Meeting Ella and Letty yesterday was exactly what I needed. Just like the day before, I lose myself in class the second our professor starts talking and the morning flies by.

Before I know it, our class is drawing to an end and I'm taking notes on our first assignment before following all the others from the auditorium and heading out of the building.

The winter sun blinds me as I step out into the coolness and suck in deep lungfuls of fresh air.

Checking my surroundings, I head in the direction that Ella and I walked from the coffee shop

I met them both in yesterday. I can't see either of them when I pull the heavy door open and step inside, so I once again join the line and order myself some lunch, my stomach growling loudly as I wait, seeing as I woke up too late to grab any food this morning.

I stayed up long after I should have, trying to get on top of yesterday's assignment and when the alarm went off this morning, I turned it off and rolled over. Needless to say, it was the wrong move and I ended up running around like a headless chicken to get here on time this morning.

With my veggie wrap and cappuccino in hand, I make my way over to an empty table for four at the back of the coffee shop and get comfortable.

I push down concerns that Ella and Letty might bail on me. They have every right to do so, we don't actually know each other, but I really want to trust them and tell myself that their class just has run over.

Sitting back in the chair, I look around at all the students eating their lunch and chatting with friends. I don't recognize anyone. It's no surprise. Aside from Ella, Letty, Luca, or Leon, I would probably struggle to recognize anyone I went to school with in Rosewood if they're here, just like I wouldn't expect anyone to give me a second glance. It's not just my hair that's different these days. I'm older, wiser, hardened to the realities of life and the pain that comes along with it. I barely recognize myself in the mirror some days, anyone else doesn't stand a chance.

Moving my eyes to the windows, I gasp in shock when they land on a very familiar figure.

Luca.

My heart jumps into my throat and my stomach knots, threatening to bring up the few mouthfuls of lunch I've already had.

He's standing with three other guys. I don't think I know any of them, but I find it hard to really focus on them because I'm still too drawn to Luca even after all these years.

His hair is shorter than it was back in high school and instead of flopping down on his brow, it's styled away from his face. His jaw is squarer, sharper, and covered in dark scruff from days of not shaving. His lips are just as full as I remember and I can't help running my tongue along my bottom one as I wonder if he still tastes the same. His nose is still straight and just the perfect size. Seriously, if football didn't work out, he could totally be a model. But what I really want to see but can't from this distance, are his eyes. They were always the most mesmerizing green. I could get lost in them for hours and I'm sure that's something that's not changed.

I'm so lost in watching him with his friends that I don't notice when Ella and Letty join me. The movement of them pulling the chairs out around me causes a small shriek to fall from my lips.

"They're pretty distracting, right?" Ella asks, her eyes locked on the same guys that mine were on only seconds ago.

"U-uh..." I stutter, really not wanting to get into anything about the reason behind my fascination. "Y-yeah. Don't tell me, they're part of the football team?"

"What gave them away?" she asks with a laugh. "The arrogance they ooze or their over-the-top confidence?"

"B-both," I confess.

Letty looks over at them, but she shows much less interest than Ella whose eyes seem to linger on one of them a little too long.

"One of them yours?" I ask Ella, the thought of her being Luca's girlfriend—or anyone being with him really—makes my stomach knot painfully.

"Pfft," she says, ripping her eyes away from them and focusing on her lunch. "All they do is fuck and chuck. Fucking pigs."

"Ignore her, she's been burned by number twenty-two," Letty chips in.

"I have not been burned, thank you very much."

"Riiight, so you don't spend most of the day looking around for him," she deadpans.

Ella's back straightens but her anger is hard to take seriously with the smirk playing on her lips.

"Oh, did you want to revisit your issues with certain members of the team, Miss Hunter?"

Ella's eyes hold Letty's for a beat before they drop

to the table. Intrigued as to what's holding her attention, I follow her stare.

"Holy crap, are you engaged to a football player?" I blurt without thought.

Letty chuckles as I admire her stunning black diamond engagement ring. I can't help but wonder the reason behind the color of the stone. It's stunning, unique and I just know there's a story there for him not to have gone for the standard.

"Yeah. Not one of those guys though."

Relief floods me. I have no say in what Luca does or who he's attached to anymore. That ship has long sailed but I can't help wanting to hear that he's not a player, that he's single, that he's held out for me.

I almost laugh out loud at my thought—okay, fantasy.

I already know it's not true, I've spent enough time scrolling through his social media over the years to know that he's always got a girl on his arm.

"Kane's... different," Ella explains, making Letty snort a laugh.

"You can say that again."

With a soft smile playing on her lips, Letty gives me the CliffsNotes of her relationship with her fiancé. The story makes my chest ache hearing about how they grew up together but spent most of their teen and young adult years at each other's throats before figuring their shit out after finding themselves at MKU together unexpectedly. I'm sure there's a hell of a lot more to the story than she lets on in her five-minute run down, but even still, it gives me hope. Probably naïvely, but my teenage heart still craves my all-American boy from the fancy house a few streets over who stole my heart with one cheeky smile.

"Sounds like you two have quite the story," I force past the giant lump in my throat.

"It wasn't love at first sight, that's for sure. So what about you? Got a boy on the scene?"

I chuckle, thinking of the boy who's taken over my life recently. "Nope. Boys are off my radar right now."

"We'll fix that Friday night, right, Let? You got the night off, right?"

"Umm..." I hesitate. "My boss wouldn't let me switch," I lie, guilt eating me as I do. I really want to make the most of this budding friendship, but equally, I don't want to be at a party where he's likely to be. The longer I can remain hidden in the shadows the better.

"Damn, girl. You're just going to have to come after. We're going to sort our costumes tomorrow after class. Wanna join?"

My lips part to refuse, but tomorrow is my night off and I'll feel like a jerk if I pass up this opportunity.

"S-sure, I'd love to," I say, not having to force the smile that appears on my face at the thought of spending time with them off campus.

"Perfect. We'll have you looking like such a goddess that all the boys will be tripping over themselves to get to you," she says, rubbing her hands together as if I've just turned into a little pet project for her.

"Uh... that's okay. I don't—"

"You can argue as much as you like," Letty interrupts. "But I should warn you that she'll still get her way."

"Hey, you make me sound like a control freak," Ella argues.

"I'm not trying to make you sound like one, you are one."

Ella huffs in frustration but movement outside the window stops me from focusing on her response to Letty.

My heart picks up speed as the guys head this way.

My pulse thunders through my body and my chest begins to heave as panic assaults me.

He can't come in here. He just can't.

I wring my trembling hands under the table, my eyes tracking the group's movement as they get closer.

My eyes flash to the only door, the one they're about to walk to.

I can't even escape.

My head spins as the thought of coming face to face with him once more in public becomes more and more a reality when he claps his hand on one of his friend's shoulders, says something briefly and then takes off in the opposite direction without looking back.

Holy fuck. That was close.

"Peyton, are you okay? You look like you've just seen a ghost."

"Oh, um... yeah, sorry. I just remembered something that I..." I trail off, not able to finish the sentence, not only because it's all a lie but because I literally can't form words as I watch his back retreat around the corner.

The realization that I need to man up and talk to him slams into me.

I'm two days into this new start and I'm already a mess.

I hoped that I'd be able to avoid him.

This campus is huge. We should be able to live entirely separate lives without ever bumping into each other. But of course that's not how this is going to work because fate is a bitch and for some reason the universe thinks that we need to be close once more.

They both look at me with concerned expressions while I fight to get myself under control.

"Everything's fine, I promise."

They both smile, but neither of them look like they believe me. Thankfully, though, they let it go. For now. I have no doubt that if this budding friendship continues then they're going to want to know more about me and if—when—Luca and I collide again, they're going to have even more questions about me seeing as he's the King of MKU. Hell, they've both probably already slept with him.

Once we've finished eating and thankfully started gossiping about things that don't involve me, my past or a certain quarterback, Ella excuses herself to her afternoon class, and Letty and I head for the library.

Thankfully, she seems to be as dedicated to her studies as I am and not much is said between us as we sit at a table together and tap away on our laptops. We work in comfortable silence and I can't help feeling more at home than I have in quite a long while, just in her presence.

I slump down in my chair, my shoulders aching from the position I'm sitting in and let out a sigh. The time is ticking by and it's impossible to forget that I've got another shift tonight.

And it's Tuesday. I silently groan. For some reason, Tuesday nights are the busiest of the week. But, while it might be crazy, it also comes with extra tips. Money is the reason I'm there, so I swallow down my dread.

"It'll get better," Letty says softly.

"Huh?" I ask, still lost in my own head about what tonight is going to hold to have a clue of what she's talking about.

"Starting over. It'll get better."

"Oh, yeah. I know. I've just got a lot of family shit going on right now. It's kinda dragging me down," I say, risking opening up to her.

"Ugh, that's the worst. Do you want to talk about it?"

The thought of telling my truths, exposing my

pain is about as terrifying as looking directly into Luca's angry eyes again.

"N-no, not really."

"Okay. Well, if you do. We're here. I know how hard it is so if there's anything I can do."

"T-thank you," I whisper, my voice cracking with emotion.

I haven't told anyone my reality. Everyone in my circle knows what happened because they've been a part of it. The thought of just saying the words shatters my heart, I can only imagine how painful it'll be when I finally run out of excuses and have to confess everything.

"I need to head out."

"Work again?"

"Always. Gotta pay for all this somehow."

"It'll be worth it in the end," she says, closing down her laptop to walk out with me. "I've got a shift tonight too while Kane's at practice." Her entire expression changes when she says his name and I can't help but smile knowing she's found that.

There have been times over the years where I thought true love and happily ever afters were a myth. I thought I had it, but it was ripped from under me before I knew what happened. We might have been young but I knew. And what if that was my only chance? Am I now destined to a life as a spinster?

I shake my head, pushing away my insecurities about my life and my future.

We chat about her job in a coffee shop and the

apartment she shares with her fiancé as we make our way to the parking lot.

"See you tomorrow for toga construction?" she says as I open my car door.

"Yeah, sounds like fun."

"If Ella is involved then you can guarantee it."

5

PEYTON

I'm filled with the same trepidation that I am every time I step out of the staff area and out into the main bar, but on a Tuesday night, it's always worse.

I've only been here a few weeks, but I already know some of the regulars, and I'm fully aware of exactly what they expect from me.

My stomach turns at the thought of what I'm going to have to do tonight to get the tips I need.

I feel their burning stares as I step out into the lights and make my way over toward Bry who's working the bar.

"Evening, gorgeous," he says, dropping his eyes down my body. "You on a mission tonight?"

"I'm always on a mission, Bry. To get out of here as soon as possible."

He chuckles at my response as he passes me a bottle of water.

"Your favorite table awaits." I take a sip of the water before stashing it on the shelf at the end of the bar for when I need a breather in about... two minutes.

"Great." I grab my notepad, not that I'll need it, they never order anything different as they sit there and strip me naked with their eyes.

Disgust rolls through me as I make my way over.

"Here's our girl," the most cringeworthy one of them says directly to my tits. He's got the bushiest eyebrows I think I've ever seen and I'm desperate to get a trimmer on them.

"Evening, gentlemen. What can I get for you tonight?" I pop my hip and lean against the booth they're sitting in, close enough to the least scary one of the group. The scent of his cologne fills my nose and my mouth goes dry.

I fucking hate this.

"You already know what we want, princess," the one with the greasy slicked back hair says.

They're all office workers and turn up on a weekly basis in their suits with their designer watches, but I can tell you that that is where their class ends. I'd put money on that all of them have wives and kids at home, yet they choose to spend their evening here getting their rocks off looking at my tits and ass and making me as uncomfortable as humanly possible with their lewd comments.

"Macallan all around then, boys?" I purr.

"Don't forget our hot wings," Eyebrows adds.

"Would I forget?"

Placing my notepad on the table, I stick my ass out as I write down their order as if I'm some dumb airhead that can't remember two things on the short walk over to the bar.

My skin prickles as they eat me up and as soon as I've finished my little show, I flash them a seductive smile and saunter off. But I don't make it back to the bar before Slick calls for me.

"We're celebrating tonight, princess, and we're feeling generous. Show us a good night and we'll make it worth your while."

My stomach churns at his words but I force a smile onto my face and retreat to the safety of the bar.

"You are aware of how much they'd probably pay you if you took them to the back room, right?" Bry asks.

"I'm not that fucking desperate," I mutter, not even needing to tell him their order. He knows as well as I do.

"Just saying, it would get you out of here quicker."

I want to be annoyed at him, but I can't. He's one of the only people who really seems to understand my need to be here despite the fact we've never shared our stories, there's just something about him that makes me think he gets it.

Helena, one of the other waitresses, approaches us. Her filled lips are painted bright red and her fake tits damn near pushed up around her neck. Resting her elbows on the bar she flashes her cleavage at Bry who pays her very little attention.

"Order's up, sweetie," she purrs, sliding her order over to him. "What's up, girl?" she asks, blatantly running her eyes over me disapprovingly.

I know I don't look like most of the other girls here. I don't have a fake thing on my body. Okay, aside from my eyelashes. I roll my eyes at myself. And while I might try my best to flirt with the customers, it's glaringly obvious that I have no idea what I'm doing and that I'm totally uncomfortable doing it. Bry tells me that that's my whole appeal, that I've got the innocent virgin vibe going on. And while I hate the thought of the men who leer at me thinking about ruining my innocence, I know it's what gets the tips and ultimately what landed me the job here in the first place.

I wish I could have just got a job at a coffee shop like Letty and serve normal people their caffeine and sugar fixes daily.

"Going for the big tips tonight, love?" Helena asks, her eyes zeroing in on my breasts, much like the men.

"Well, I might not have as much as you, but I figure I should work with what I've got."

Bry snorts a laugh, quickly covering it up with a cough, but it's too late, Helena heard it loud and clear.

"Well, enjoy the tips you can get. When you're ready to play with the women, you just let me know."

She spins around with her notebook poised, ready to take more orders from her adoring customers when Bry calls her back.

"Helena."

"Yes," she hisses, clearly done with both of us.

"You've got a little..." He taps the corner of his mouth. "Cum, maybe."

"Oh my God," I cry as her face twists in frustration. She storms off to the sound of our laughter.

"She's going to kill you with the heel of her stiletto," I tell him once she's out of earshot.

"Meh, it would be worth it. She's a bitch. I'd have you over her any day of the week."

"Bry, you're gay."

"Yeah, I'm not fucking blind though." He drops his eyes down my mostly exposed body and I can't help it heating up with his attention.

"Stop it," I snap.

"I fucking knew it. You want a bit of this, don't you?" he says, lifting his shirt to show off his abs.

"Ew, as if. I have no idea where you've been."

"In some really, really fucked up guys," he deadpans.

"Ah, got a thing for the bad boys, do you?" I ask as he continues to put me off, grabbing the glasses I need for my table of assholes.

"Who doesn't?"

My lips part to argue but the words die on my tongue.

Luca was vicious that first night, but fuck if he didn't call to me even more so than he did back in the day. The wicked glint in his eyes, the snarl on his lips. Hell, if I'd have turned him down.

"Yeah, alright. You gonna finish this for me before they expect extras for me being late."

"Yes." He turns his back on me and grabs the glasses before sliding the tray over. "Pey," he says when I take off, holding the tray with one hand over my shoulder.

"Yeah."

"Be careful with those guys, I don't like the way they look at you."

"I've got this, Bry. You don't need to worry about me." I put as much confidence into my voice as possible, covering the fact on the inside I'm a terrified wreck who would rather hide in a dark closet than serve those sleazy jerks. But that's not going to pay the medical bills that are racking up faster than I can cope with.

Throwing my shoulders back and holding my head up high, I make my way over.

As expected, under the disgusting stares of the regulars, my night drags. Even the banter with Bry doesn't turn my night around, and by the time my shift comes to an end, I can't run out of the building fast enough.

Thankfully, my fan club left about fifteen minutes ago, allowing me to step out of the back door of the club without too much concern about them still being back here. From the amount they all put away, there's no way they should be anywhere near a car anyway.

But as I take my first steps toward my car, I can't ignore the shiver that races down my spine.

The majority of the parking lot is illuminated by the security lights lining the building, but there are still plenty of dark spots that someone could hide in if they wanted to.

My eyes fly around in the hope of seeing whatever it is that's making all my hairs stand on end, but I don't see anyone. The parking lot is mostly empty, just a couple of the regular's cars who are still inside along with the remaining staff.

Swallowing down my fear, I continue forward. I tell myself that it's just the memory of the way those men looked at me tonight that has me on edge, but still, I don't believe it.

Someone is watching me.

Someone is—

The scream that erupts from my throat when a hot body presses against my back not a second later is cut off when a hand wraps around my mouth.

I'm shoved forward as my heart pounds so hard in my chest that I feel it in my toes.

My entire body trembles with fear.

Stupid, stupid girl, I think to myself. I knew I was

playing with fire tonight in the hope of getting more tips, but all I've done is make them think they could take whatever they wanted.

I whimper beneath the hand as a strong arm wraps around my waist and I'm lifted from the ground.

I manage to get a look at the arm around me and even in the dull light, it's clear to see that it's not a suit jacket or even a shirt.

The man who has me is wearing a hoodie.

Oh God.

Together we slip into the darkness and somehow my pulse picks up even more speed knowing that even if someone did come back here, they'd never see us.

The front of my body presses up against a car and his long, hard body pins me in place.

"You didn't think I'd forgotten, did you?" a familiar voice growls in my ear.

The shudder of fear immediately turns into something else entirely as his breath caresses my ear and down my neck. Despite his obvious anger, there's still something there that calls to me, that feels right. Although everything about this is so very, very wrong.

I whimper again, wishing I was able to say something, anything, to get me out of this right now.

"I've been watching you, you know. Watching you leave every night. Wondering exactly who you've spent the night shaking your ass at for some cash."

Emotion clogs my throat, shame washing through

me for the depths I've lowered myself to. Only a few months ago, I never would have considered a job like this. But needs must and all that.

"I guess it's true what they say, the apple never falls far from the tree."

No, I want to scream.

I know what people thought of my mom. I spent years having to endure the guys ribbing me over her job. But that's all it was. A job. A job to ensure that her girls had a roof over their heads and food in their bellies.

I don't want to hear anything bad about the woman who gave her life to look after us.

Suddenly, I'm moving. My front leaves the car and I'm spun around until it's my back against the cool metal.

Luca's hand leaves my mouth, his fingers curling around the top of his car and pinning me in.

"Don't even think about calling for help, Little Girl."

A weird mix of comfort and hatred races through me at his use of the name he used to call me all those years ago. It was always a joke because I was a couple of weeks younger than him. But right now, it feels anything like a joke and everything like a threat.

I am little compared to him. I always was. But in our time apart he's grown, both in height and bulk, and I already know that I don't stand a chance against him.

My lips part, but no noise passes them, just a

large exhale as I stare into his dark eyes. I know they're the most incredible green, but right now, hidden in the darkness, it's hard to see.

He stares at me as if he can't believe I'm actually standing before him.

His chest heaves, his full lips parted as he fights to keep his cool.

"You shouldn't have come back here," he warns, his voice low and cold in a way I remember all too well from the last time we spoke.

"I-I—"

"No," he barks. "I don't want your pity story, Peyton."

I swallow down the argument that was on the tip of my tongue, although I already know that it was weak at best because there is no way I'm telling him the truth. I'm not giving him any more ammunition to hurt me than he already thinks he has.

"Did you think you would turn up here and I wouldn't find you?"

I stare at him, willing him to see the truth in my eyes.

I didn't have any other option.

"Or is that exactly what you wanted? That I would find you and that I'd have forgotten? Did you think that I'd put all your lies behind me and that we could just pick back up where we left off?" He spits the words as if even saying them disgusts him. "Did you really miss me that much?"

Internally, I scream yes. Yes, I really missed him

that much. When we first moved away, I'd have done anything to have my best friend back. Literally anything. But I knew there was no way it was going to happen. Just like I don't think it's going to happen now either.

"Let's see what you've had on offer tonight then. See if we can make all of this worthwhile for me."

"W-wha—"

I'm frozen in shock as he lifts his hand to the zipper on the front of my hoodie and pulls it down.

Unlike last night, this one actually belongs to me. The moment I put it on, I missed the comfort of Elijah's. It's crazy but it's like some weird security blanket.

The cool winter air washes over my exposed skin, making me shiver. That is until his eyes drop from mine and scorch a trail over my skin.

Then I'm burning up. My blood boiling from the inside from the way that he's making me feel.

But it's not for him. It's not lust or my desire for him to touch me.

It's shame.

Red hot shame for the person I've become, the woman he's standing before after all these years and what I've lowered myself to.

It's no surprise he doesn't like me. Every time I come to this place and put in a shift, I hate myself a little bit more.

It's just a means to an end, I tell myself. My family needs me, and this is the best way I can help.

But that knowledge doesn't make it any better.

A growl of disapproval rumbles at the back of his throat before he clicks his tongue.

"You were showing those boys a good time tonight, huh?" he mutters.

Unable to even look at him as he judges me, I turn my head to the side and stare into the darkness, wishing like hell that it would swallow me up.

Why did it have to be like this?

The lump in my throat is so large, it's hard to even breathe as he continues studying me.

"Tell me..." he starts, making my stomach sink for what's going to come next. "Did you make a lot of tips tonight?"

I don't answer him. I don't even look at him. Too mortified by the knowledge of just how much I made from merely showing off a little too much skin.

Not happy with my lack of response, Luca shoves his hand into the pocket of my hoodie, correctly guessing where I stashed the cash.

"Fucking hell," he gasps when he pulls the wad of bills out. "What did you do tonight, you filthy slut?" he growls, leaning in and whispering in my ear.

"N-nothing."

"Bullshit," he spits, moving closer still. We're not touching but the heat of his skin burns. It makes me tingle with my need for him to actually touch me. To know if it's still as electric as it was back then.

When he does finally connect with me, it's not at

all in the way I'd hoped, or longed for, after all these years.

I swallow down the whimper that wants to erupt when his hot fingers wrap around my throat.

They squeeze lightly in warning, making my eyes burn with red hot tears.

I'm sorry. I'm so sorry, I scream internally, knowing full well that what happened between us was what created—or at least contributed to—the angry, vicious, dark boy who's standing before me. He was always there, hiding under the surface. Whenever someone pissed him off—mainly his dad— he would emerge. But only ever behind closed doors, and only ever alone or with me or Leon. His safe places.

What the rest of the world saw when shit hit the fan was an entirely different person to the one I knew. He was ashamed of the place he went when he was really angry, and I knew why, even without him ever telling me.

It made him like his father.

His temper, his ability to lash out. It was just like Brett Dunn, and Luca hated it.

I got it. His dad was a douchebag of epic proportions. I just always wished he found a way to deal with it instead of hiding and taking it out on those he loved. Me, Lee, his mom.

It makes me wonder if anyone else has been there for him over the past five years with me gone.

My heart aches considering that there might be a

woman out there right now who understands this side of him. Who helps him through it much like I used to.

"Don't act like a stupid little girl, Peyton. We both know you're not. And, we both know exactly what happens in there to earn this kind of money. So... What. Did. You. Do?"

"N-nothing," I repeat.

"Who touched you?"

"N-no one." It's not entirely true. Slick did get a little handsy after the fourth bottle of whisky was delivered to their table, but he didn't touch me like I'm sure Luca is thinking right now.

He shakes his head at me, disappointment rolling off him in waves.

"So, all this money just to look, huh? They must really think you're something special."

"I-I'm nothing, Luc. I just... I just give them what they want."

"Trust me. If you didn't let them touch you, if you didn't touch them, I can assure you that you got nowhere fucking close to giving them what they wanted."

I swallow down my response because we both know any argument I might have would be a lie.

"You're a tease, Peyton. Walking around like this, giving guys ideas." His eyes drop to my breasts, and even in the dark, I know exactly what he can see and it makes me want the ground to swallow me whole.

My hands curl into tight fists and I squeeze my

eyes closed, wishing that I were anywhere but here right now. That we could have collided again in any other place than this. Any other time than tonight.

"Tell me, P. Were these as hard for them as they are for me right now?"

I gasp when his soft touch brushes over one of my nipples.

His fingers tighten around my throat when I don't immediately respond.

"I-It's the cold."

"Fucking bullshit, P. We both know that if I were to push my hand inside your panties right now that you'd be dripping fucking wet for me."

My eyes fly up to his in shock. His words rocking me to my very core and reminding me that I'm not dealing with a sixteen-year-old Luca anymore. I'm dealing with a man with more anger and hurt than I know how to navigate.

"Wait..." he says before I have any time to fight my corner. "You are wearing panties, right? You're not that desperate for those cunts' money that you've been bending over in this short skirt all night and showing them what's mine."

"Y-yours?" I stutter, ignoring the rest of his statement. My shock at his ownership of my body too much to brush aside.

A low, menacing chuckle rumbles up his throat. A terrifying smirk curls at his lips.

"Yeah, Peyton. *Mine.*"

I swallow, trying to force down the ever-growing

lump, but it's pointless. Even long after he releases me, I know it's going to remain.

I hold his eyes, dragging up as much confidence as I can muster while refusing to dignify his question with an actual answer.

That all goes to shit though when he lowers his hand, skimming his knuckles along the edge of my skirt.

"Yes. Yes," I cry. "I'm wearing panties."

Pulling his hand away, he lifts the cash he's still got in his fingers.

His lips curl once more before he pushes it all into the pocket of his sweats.

"Luca, please. I need—"

"What you need is to stop looking like a cheap whore, P."

"It's my job. I need the money."

"Tell me why and maybe I'll go easier on you. Assuming I believe a word that comes out of your lying mouth."

6

LUCA

My heart is a runaway train in my chest as I stare into her silver eyes, watching her internal battle. She wants to tell me her reasons for being here because she wants to get away, I don't need to be able to feel the tremor wracking her body to know that she's scared of me right now, I can practically taste her fear and it feeds some part of me that I wasn't aware needed sating quite so badly.

I knew standing before her, looking into her eyes was going to calm the war raging inside me. But I had no idea her fear was going to be this... addictive.

"Tell me," I demand again as footsteps in the gravel of the parking lot sound out. I have no idea if it's some of tonight's late-night customers or staff, I don't rip my eyes from Peyton's to find out.

I don't need to say anything to warn her against

calling out or asking for help. She seems to know that it would be a really bad fucking thing to do.

She swallows once more, her delicate skin rippling against my hand, making me want to tighten my hold to terrify her even more. But I resist, for now.

I still want to address the fact that even in the fucking dark I can clearly see the imprint of her nipples through her shirt and why she thought for even a second that it was a good idea to step outside of the house looking like that, let alone spend the night around the disgusting cunts who spend their Tuesday nights at The Locker Room.

"Fuck you, Luc. I owe you nothing. What I do has nothing to do with you. You made your place in my life very clear five years ago. You don't get to storm back in now and shame me for doing what I need to do."

Her fire makes my cock swell. It always took a lot to rattle her. I think that's one of the reasons we just worked so well. Whenever I'd lose my shit, she'd always been the one to cool me off, to make me see things from a different perspective. I can probably count on one hand the number of times I saw her angry. The worst of those times was the last time I saw her.

Memories of that afternoon still haunt me. But I did the right thing. I couldn't let her poison me with her lies. Even if she had no idea they were lies.

A huge part of me knows that she doesn't really

believe it, that she's just putting too much loyalty on those she loves.

What infuriated me back then, and still does now, is that she had the audacity to stand there and make those bullshit claims as if she actually believed it.

What she told me... it was... it was serious.

There's no way... no fucking way...

"What the hell are you doing?" she hisses when I lift my hand once more and gently rub at her nipple through the thin fabric of her shirt with the pad of my thumb.

"Did you even look in a mirror before you stepped out in this?" I ask, my eyes locked on my movements as her peak hardens even more with the sensation.

I'm not the only one who's changed since the last time we saw each other. She was a young woman back then. Now she's all woman. The curves she's developed threaten to fucking ruin me. Sadly for her, the only one here who's getting ruined is her.

I've waited years to finally have this out between us and now she's right here.

My prey.

She keeps her lips pressed into a thin line, refusing to speak after her little outburst.

"So I'll assume you did then and you wanted every man in that place to imagine how they look bare. If your nipples are as pink and rosy as they're imagining. I bet they were wondering just how you would sound if they were to—"

Her gasp of shock rips through the air as I pinch down hard on her sensitive peak.

Her eyes narrow in warning but it's impossible to miss how much they darken at my move.

"You like that, P? Is what you were hoping for? For someone to take away that innocence you seem to be trying to convince everyone of with this little act."

Leaning forward, I brush my lips against her ear.

"Is that it? Have you told them all that you're a virgin?"

A growl vibrates up her throat. I'd miss it if I weren't holding her so tight.

"Just another lie to add to all the others you spill because we both know you're anything but a virgin, don't we, P?"

Her chest heaves as she stares at me. Memories of us together, figuring each other's bodies out all those years ago, are almost visible in her gray depths.

"How much do you think they'd pay you for this?" I ask, switching to the other side which is already at a hard point for me.

She shakes her head, still trying to claim her innocence.

"What about a taste, P? How much does that cost?"

"I don't sell my body, Luc." The plea in her voice only makes me want to push her more. And I realize for the first time just how much I want to break her.

Just like she broke me.

Everything changed for me the day her mom

dragged her out of Rosewood. My trust was in tatters, my life imploding on me, and everything I thought I knew was in question.

I've trusted no one with the darkest part of me since that day.

I found a vault deep inside and locked it all down because I couldn't risk anyone betraying me like that again.

Letty thinks she knows everything about me. But she doesn't. There are parts that I've never exposed to her. Parts that even Leon hasn't seen for a very long time.

They both just think I'm a little hot-headed, and I am, I can't deny that. But it's what happens when I lock myself into my room after that outburst that they have no idea about.

Peyton knows it all though. She's seen every dark and twisted side of me and despite knowing that, she fucking broke me.

"You're fucking right there. You've already taken enough from me. It's time for me to repay the favor."

Releasing her throat, I wrap my fingers around the cropped hem of her shirt and push it up, exposing her bare tits.

They're fucking perfect and everything I've spent years dreaming about but like fuck am I about to tell her that.

Before she has a chance to protest, I lower down and suck one into my mouth.

Her sweetness explodes in my mouth and my cock weeps for her.

I remember the image of her lips wrapped around my length all too well. I remember her hesitation, her nerves. It makes me wonder how much more confidence she might have now. How much practice she might have had.

The thought of her on her knees for some other motherfucker makes my fists clench but I soon realize I've something better right before me to release my frustration on.

"Luc," she cries as I bite down on the nipple deep in my mouth as I pinch the other.

Her fingers thrust into my hair, pulling hard and making my scalp sting as she tries to fight me off.

"And to think, you tried to deny being a whore," I mutter against the fullness of her breast.

"I'm not. Get the hell off me."

"Stop lying to yourself, P. You want this. You're wet for this."

"No. I hate you, Luc. I fucking hate you."

Her words send a tsunami of anger racing through me.

"You hate me?" I roar, forgetting all about where we are and that anyone could hear and come rushing to her rescue. My hand finds her throat once more but my grip is much more brutal this time and her eyes widen in fear. Once upon a time, she'd have every confidence in me never taking things too far, never hurting her. But times have fucking changed and she deserves all the pain I can deliver. "I did nothing, P. Fucking nothing," I bellow, the hurt sixteen-year-old boy inside me rearing his little head. "You ruined everything with your bullshit lies. I loved you, P. I loved you so fucking much and you fucking broke me."

Need, hunger, anger, depravity, it all swirls around me like a dark cloud making me forget who I really am, where we are and what I should be doing.

"Luca, no," Peyton cries as I rip her panties aside. Kicking her legs wider with my feet, I sink two fingers deep inside her. Her velvet heat surrounds me and immediately something settles because I was right.

I was fucking right.

"Fuck, P. You're fucking dripping right now."

"Luca," she whimpers but her body is clearly on a different page than her head because as I bend my fingers inside her, she clamps down on me, a rush of liquid running down my digits and to my hand.

"You enjoy walking around looking like a filthy slut, don't you? Does it make you feel powerful knowing that all the men want you?"

"No," she cries.

"Let's make a deal."

She thrashes her head from side to side trying to ignore what my fingers are doing buried deep inside her.

"We'll let them look... for now. But no one else touches what's mine."

"Luc." Her voice is raspy, her body teetering right on the edge of her release.

The need to push her over. To watch her fall once again because of me is almost too much to deny.

Almost.

"Oh shit. Luc. No," she cries, sagging against the side of my car as I rip my fingers from inside her.

Her chest heaves, her nipples still glistening from my attention. Her eyes are blown and I know if I could see better her cheeks and chest would be bright red with her almost-release.

Lifting my hand, I make the most of her parted lips and push them inside.

"Suck them clean."

Her eyes widen once more in surprise but whatever she sees in mine ensures she does as she's told.

I damn near come in my pants like a fucking schoolboy when her tongue laves at me.

Grinding my teeth, I rip my fingers away again.

"Good girl." I take a step back and she sags lower, her knees barely holding her up. "I meant what I said, P. No one else touches you." Bending to her height, I look into her eyes so she can see how serious I am. "Even your cunt of a boyfriend." The word is bitter on my tongue but I can't leave it unsaid after seeing them yesterday.

"My b-boy—" She slams her lips shut, probably realizing that I really have been watching her. She swallows nervously.

"Now, get off my car. You're making it look cheap."

Her jaw drops in shock as I wrap my hand around the fabric of her hoodie and pull her away.

She stumbles back away from me, wrapping it around herself to cover up.

It's a damn shame but I'll let it go. For now.

"Luc, wait. Please."

I take two steps toward the driver's door before I realize what she's begging for.

Digging my hand into my pocket, I pull out her cash, along with my wallet.

"This all you care about?" I say, throwing the bills at her.

She wants to look down, to gather them up, but she doesn't. Her eyes remain on mine, begging me to stop.

She can try that all she wants. What she really needs to realize is that this is just the beginning.

Opening my wallet, I stare her straight in the eyes when I ask my next question. "So how much for the fingerbang?"

A garbled cry falls from her lips and I pull a few bills from my wallet. I have no idea how much is in there but I really don't give a fuck.

I throw the money at her before ripping my car door open and dropping into the seat.

I look in the mirror as I pull out of the lot and find her in a pile on the ground with her head in her hands.

My stomach knots. The little boy within me wanting to go and scoop up the girl who was his entire life. To help her put the pieces back together and tell her that everything is going to be okay.

But he's long gone. The man in his place is nowhere near as caring to the person who killed that sweet boy.

7

PEYTON

Tears continue to cascade down my cheeks as I make the drive back to Aunt Fee's house. My body trembles as those few moments with Luca play on repeat in my head. Every vicious word taunts me, every barbed insult and insinuation about being a whore hurt more and more every time I hear them. Yet, despite all of that, my skin still burns from where he touched me. My core muscles tighten with the memory of his fingers inside me.

I was so close. So close to just forgetting about my reality for just a few seconds and he took it from me.

A sob erupts as I pull to a stop outside the house.

I can't walk in there like this, Aunt Fee will take one look at me and demand to know what's wrong.

I could lie, sure. I've got enough to cry about in my life right now, but she'd see straight through it. She'd know that this was different. It is. It's different because it's about him. The only person I've ever given my heart to.

Instead of turning the engine off, I throw the car back into drive and pull off again.

I can't sit out here in case one of them notices, and I can't walk inside until I've got myself under control.

I drive around town, wishing that I was back in Rosewood and that I could go and sit on the beach. Listening to the crashing waves is perfect when you need to get out of your own head.

Luc and I used to spend hours down on the beach after dark just laying on the cool sand putting the world to rights.

My chest tightens. What I wouldn't give to go back to easier times with him.

I find a coffee shop with a drive-thru in the center of town and order myself the biggest hot chocolate with all the trimmings that they have before pulling into the parking lot, sliding my chair back and just allowing myself a moment to breathe.

My time with Luca was intense. Part of me is surprised by his brutality, his need to hurt me. But another part isn't. I've seen that side of him before. But in the past, it was only ever directed at his dad or occasionally an opposing player who touched a sore spot. It was never—other than just before I left—been directed at me quite like that.

A shiver races up my spine as I think about his electric touch. Although vicious and tinged with hate, it was exactly as I hoped it would be. The second he brushed his thumb over my nipple, the same electric sparks I remember all too well zipped through my body, assaulting my nerve endings.

My nipples harden once more, the throb in my clit returning from my lost orgasm. Resting my head back, I close my eyes and blow out a long, slow breath. I can almost feel the ghost of his fingers still deep inside me.

My head flies up as I realize what I'm doing.

What the fuck is wrong with me?

I didn't want that. I didn't ask for that. Why am I sitting here fantasizing about it?

Shaking my head, my cheeks burn red hot in the knowledge that I'd have let that continue tonight, and possibly so much more given the chance.

It didn't matter the malicious words he'd spat at me. I was with Luca again. Something about his presence just spoke to my soul.

He knew it too.

It's why he played me like he did.

My hot chocolate is long gone by the time I start the engine once more, feeling like I'm going to be able to walk through Aunt Fee's front door and not give myself away instantly.

I don't realize just how late it is until I pull back up outside the house and notice that it's in darkness.

It's not often that Aunt Fee heads to bed before I'm home, but clearly, she got bored with waiting tonight.

With a heavy heart and a knot that seems to be a permanent fixture in the pit of my stomach, I head inside.

The house is as quiet as I expected, and I tiptoe down the hallway toward the kitchen to grab a glass of water to take upstairs with me.

I'm standing at the sink, staring at my reflection in the window before me, still questioning myself over how I felt tonight with Luca when a voice makes me drop the glass in my hand.

"Holy sh—moly," I curse when I spin around and see a small face looking at me with his brows drawn in concern. "You scared me, baby boy."

His lips twist in the way they always do when I call him that.

"You're late," he states.

"Err... yeah, I got held up. You should be asleep," I warn.

"I know." He stares at me with sad eyes. "I was waiting for you."

"I'm sorry. You're okay though, right?"

He nods, but the sadness never leaves his face. I understand why. I feel the same pain on a daily basis too.

"Come on, let's get you to bed."

I help him back to his room and tuck him in.

"I don't like you working late, Pey."

"I know, baby. But sometimes we have to do things we don't like. It will get better, I promise."

"I miss her," he says, his soft voice cracking with emotion and shattering my heart all over again.

"I know, baby. I know."

I hold his small hand in mine, allowing his warmth to ground me. He holds my eyes for a minute but they soon become too heavy once more and he drifts off to sleep.

I watch him for a long time as he snores lightly, his raggedy lamb tucked under his head.

As I sit there, I make him the promise I have done a million times over in the last couple of weeks.

I promise to make everything okay. I promise to give you everything they couldn't.

With tears in my eyes, I drop a kiss to his forehead and slip silently out of the room.

While I might have been through hell in the past few months, that little boy has had it even worse.

All of this is for him. All of it.

I'll take everything Luca throws my way. All his vicious accusations and wicked touches because Kayden is my endgame here. He's lost too much for me to give up on him too.

I arrive at Ella's dorm later than I agreed because, after the night before, I knew I needed to have dinner at home.

It would be too easy to get swept up into college life while working as many hours as physically possible. But that's not my life now. I have responsibilities, and that little boy needs me.

I knew it was the right decision the second I stepped foot into the house after class and saw his little face light up.

He was working on his phonics with Aunt Fee, but she called time on their little lesson so the two of us could hang out.

He talked my ear off the entire time and then insisted on sitting beside me while we ate. It was like he was scared that if he even looked away for a second then I might vanish.

I got it. Hell, I more than got it. There were times in the past few weeks where I felt exactly the same.

Not wanting to disappoint him, I stayed and put him to bed. And I'm so glad I did. It was the reminder I needed for why I'm doing this. For why I'm putting myself through bullshit like last night.

I shudder, still able to feel the eyes of those guys on my skin.

I scrubbed every inch of my body twice as I stood under the scorching heat of Aunt Fee's shower once I left Kayden last night.

I told myself that I was washing Luca off me, but it was all lies. While a huge part of me might hate him for how he treated me, there was something about his scent clinging to my skin that just felt so right.

He might have been vicious, but I also know that

while he's watching me, the other men can't touch me. Or at least, that's what I hope anyway.

I knock on the door to Ella's dorm before pushing it open and poking my head inside.

"Well, well, well," a guy says, immediately turning his stare on me. "What do we have here?"

My skin burns as the other two guys in the room hear his comment and also turn to look at me.

"Uh..."

"Don't even try it," a familiar voice barks from the end of the room.

After a beat, Ella emerges haphazardly wrapped in a bedsheet and gives each of them a look they probably should be scared of.

"Damn, girl. You are looking—"

"Finish that sentence and lose a testicle." She pops a hip, putting a hand on her waist.

"Jeez, who pissed in your margarita?" one of them growls.

"Peyton," she says, a smile turning up the corners of her mouth when she looks over at me. "This is West, Brax, and Micah. They're something akin to our dorm pets."

I snort a laugh at the incredulous looks on two of their faces.

"Hey," I squeak, trying to keep my amusement locked down.

"She's off-limits to you pigs, so only engage the brains in your heads, please."

"Not sure these two have anything up there," the

one who's been the least interested in my arrival deadpans.

"Fuck you, man."

"Jesus. Come on." Ella holds her arm out and gestures for me to follow her.

I hear the hysterical laughter before I get to her room, and when we walk through, I discover Letty sitting on the bed with tears rolling down her cheeks while another girl that I've yet to meet is rolling around on the floor wrapped in a bedsheet.

"What the hell happened?" Ella demands.

"I think your margarita is too strong," Letty says innocently.

"When isn't it?" the other asks, finally getting to her feet, leaving the bedsheet behind and confidently standing in just her white strapless bra and panties.

"Hey, I'm Violet," she says with a smile.

"Uh... hey. I'm Pe—"

"Peyton. I've heard all about you, Pink. I think you're going to fit right in with this bunch of reprobates."

"You're aware that includes you, right, Vi?" Ella asks with a laugh, filling an empty glass from the pitcher sitting on the side and offering it over to me.

"I'm driving," I say, not taking it.

"It's okay, it's virgin for you and Letty."

"Oh, well. Thank you."

"Come sit down. Ella promised us mad skills with this but all I've seen so far is a girl wrapped in a bedsheet." She glances over at Ella, who admittedly does look exactly as she described.

"Don't worry, I've got it. Right, Vi? You remember last year? I'm just finding my flow."

She flips open a pink box and pulls out a huge pair of scissors.

"I really hope she knows what she's doing with them."

"Me too," Letty whispers back. "But at least Vi is first."

"Yes, but just how many margaritas is she going to have had by the time she gets to us?"

Letty's lips part to say something but she quickly realizes that I'm right. "Shit."

It's well past midnight when I leave their dorm with a sheet and firm instructions on how to wear it come Friday night. My face hurts from laughing so much.

I can't remember the last time that happened.

I cast my mind back but come up blank for anything over the past five years.

Memories from before I left Rosewood hit me. Laughing with Luca. Acting like complete idiots until we laughed so hard we couldn't breathe.

A smile curls at my lips thinking of those two young kids who were still naïve about real life and just loving every day.

I'd give anything to go back to then. To running

around the backyard with water pistols, to making dens and camping out overnight. To thinking that what the two of us shared would never break.

How wrong were we?

Everyone is once again asleep when I get home. Knowing that I was just hanging out with friends instead of working, Aunt Fee told me that she'd be able to relax properly, knowing I was safe. As much as I love her concern, I wish I wasn't putting any more stress on her shoulders. She's already had her life changed enough by us turning up here, I don't want to do anything to make it worse.

Unlike the night before, I fall asleep with a little bit of hope filling my veins. Things with Luca might be fucked up beyond belief, but I've actually made some friends. Some friends who might just be able to make my life here more bearable.

8

LUCA

Not going to sit in the parking lot of The Locker Room last night was weird. It's become something of a sanctuary for me over the past couple of weeks. Just seeing her walk out of the building and to her car settled something inside me. But that was nothing compared to the feeling of standing in front of her Tuesday night.

My fists curl as I walk toward my morning class with my need for a repeat.

Her scent. Her taste. The little whimpers that involuntarily fell from her lips as I brought her right to the edge, they're all I can think about.

My cock swells as the image of her pressed up against my car, her tits exposed and my hand disappearing up her skirt fills my mind.

Fuck. I really needed that last night. But, watching her the past couple of weeks, I knew that it was her night off.

The hallway is empty as I make my way down to the elevator. I'm hardly surprised. I got sucked into the gym this morning and it wasn't until one of the coaching staff poked his head in to say something that I realized the time.

I needed the release. I needed something other than my own right hand that was doing very fucking little to take the edge off.

I need her.

Reaching down, I palm my growing cock, rearranging myself so I'm not about to walk into class, not only late but with a raging boner over the girl I should have forgotten long ago.

Hitting the call button for the elevator, I step inside and slam my hand down on the button for the correct floor.

Leaning against the back wall, I close my eyes as the doors shut, shutting me off from the rest of campus for just a little bit.

Right before the doors close, I hear a curse before the doors audibly stop moving.

Blowing out a breath that someone is about to ruin my peace, I rip my head from the wall and look to see who's joined me.

She glances up at the same time I do and we both suck in a sharp breath.

"Letty," I breathe.

"Shit." Her eyes widen in surprise and she quickly takes a step back but she's too late. The doors have already closed, caging us in together. "Um... hhow are you?"

I stare at her, my heart aching in my chest.

I hate how things turned out between us. I hate that she's now with that jerk. But what can I really do about it? She was never meant to be mine. I think deep down I always knew that, but I really wanted to believe that she was here for me.

Turns out fate had other ideas because she just put her and Kane in the same place, allowing them to sort their shit out. Although not before making me want to end the motherfucker for the way he treated her. And I know for a fact that I only know the basics of the situation.

Reaching up, I wrap my hand around the back of my neck as she steps into the enclosed space a little more.

The elevator jolts as we begin our ascent, and her scent fills my nose.

"I-I'm good. You?" I hate the awkwardness, and I know that most of it—hell, all of it—is because of me.

"Y-yeah. Things are really good." Unable to stop it, a soft smile spreads across her face, I assume, as she thinks about Kane.

Asshole.

"I'm glad."

We fall into an uncomfortable silence and I hate it. I hate everything that's happened between us. After Peyton left Rosewood all those years ago, Letty turned up like a fucking angel. I was in a bad place when our teacher decided that I'd be the perfect partner for the new girl. Fuck knows what he was thinking. Maybe he hoped she'd be a good influence on me because hell knows I was fucking up all over the place back then. Even my place on the team was at risk at one point when I was caught skipping, preferring to go to the beach to get fucked up instead of dealing with the fact I'd been betrayed and abandoned by my best friend.

My lips part to say something, but I can't find the words I want to say to her. An apology doesn't seem enough after all the shit I've put her through.

She's tried to reach out to me time and time again, and I've only pushed her farther away. It's probably best for her in the long run if I do.

I think it's pretty obvious that Kane and I are never going to see eye to eye, and I'm not sure where that leaves a friendship between us.

"Luc?" she whispers after what feels like the longest silence of my life.

Dragging my eyes from my feet, I look at her. My breath catches at how happy she looks, despite the concern that's currently causing a frown to mar her brow.

"I-I'm sorry," I whisper, utterly defeated where Letty is concerned.

Her eyes hold mine. The sparkle that was within them when she first stepped into the elevator has vanished, replaced with worry, pity even, and I hate it.

"Luc, it's—"

I suck in a breath waiting to hear the words I don't deserve from her when the doors open and reveal a large group of students waiting to get inside.

Silently, we move past the group and make our way down to our lit class.

Seeing as we're both late, the professor has already started and we both slip inside and find the first two empty seats we can, side by side.

It's the closest I've been to her in weeks, and I can't deny that it feels good to have her there.

Everything in my life is fucked beyond belief right now. I know most of that is my fault, and that the situation we've found ourselves in is entirely on me. But I'm starting to wonder if it's time to put it all behind me. Letty is the least of my concerns now that Peyton is in town.

She's happy. I can see that without even having to ask her. A few weeks ago, I was drowning in jealousy that she'd found in Kane what I wanted to give her.

I have no idea what our professor is saying, and seeing as it's our first class of the semester, I really should be paying attention. With the season over, it's time for me to get some credits in the bag but I can't find it in me to focus.

My plan was always to graduate before I started playing pro football. It's just a shame that wasn't everyone's plan for me.

If Dad had his way, I'd be in this year's draft. First pick, obviously. But even if I did enter this year, I never would have been first after the season we just saw the back of.

It was embarrassing, and I know the responsibility for the clusterfuck lands on my shoulders. All the guys are pissed. I can see that just from looking at them. None of them have outwardly blamed me, but I know they do.

I fucked up. I dropped the ball—literally and figuratively. I totally lost sight of what was important as Kane stole the girl from under my feet.

But she was never my girl, was she?

I blow out a long, frustrated breath and slump down in the chair.

Movement to my side catches my eye and when I glance over, I find Letty studying me, her brows pulled together.

"Everything is going to be okay, Luc." She gives me a soft smile that I wish would make me feel better but all it does is make my chest ache for the way I treated her.

She reaches over and takes my hand. It's not an unusual move but the heat of her fingers against my skin makes my entire body jolt.

Not missing my reaction, she hesitantly pulls her hand back, muttering an apology as she does.

Every muscle in my body locks up tight as I stare at the door, my need to storm out and put all this bullshit behind me is strong.

I have no idea what I'm doing right now. Football, college, Letty, Leon, fucking Peyton.

I relax slightly just at the thought of her name. She's the only one who makes it all go away.

When I look at her, standing before her, everything else that's falling apart in my life goes quiet.

Dad's voice disappears, and all my failings as a friend, a captain, a teammate, a brother, all vanish.

It's just me and her. It's like I'm a kid again without the pressure of real life, only that my best friend is no longer that. She's a girl who lied to me. Betrayed me. And the fun we used to have together has morphed into my need to hurt her, to show her what her words, her accusations, did to me back then.

Aside from Leon who was existing in the same hell as me, she was the only one who got me. The only one who knew what my life was really like. The only one who knew how hard I battled with family issues and how badly I wanted things to be different.

And then she shattered all of it.

The pencil that was in my hand snaps under the pressure of my grip, the splintered wood digging into my skin.

My heart races as I stare down at it, feeling exactly like I did the day she dropped the bomb on me.

The auditorium around me blurs as I fight to get a grip on reality.

"Luc?" A warm hand lands on mine and fingers begin to pry mine open.

Her scent fills my nose and I blink a few times as Letty's image clears before me.

I glance around, finding that the seats are almost empty around me and the professor is nowhere to be seen.

Fuck.

"Come on, I'm buying you a coffee and a cupcake. And don't even think about arguing with me."

Even if I wanted to, I couldn't right now.

The darkness from my past is clawing at me, threatening to consume me.

I once again look around the room, willing her to appear to put it all to rest, but she never does. Instead, students just leave, too many casting curious glances my way.

When I still don't move, Letty wraps her hand around my bicep and does her best attempt at pulling me from the chair.

My lip curls up in a smile as I watch her efforts.

Blowing a lock of hair from her face, she looks up at me, exasperated.

"You're gonna need to help."

Running my eyes down her body, I'm relieved to see that she's finally putting some decent weight on. When I first ran into her at the beginning of the fall semester, she was skin and bones. But even with all the drama of the past few months, she seems to have managed to find the time to look after herself, or more likely—and I hate to even admit this—Kane has.

I might not like him. I might not trust him or

think he's good enough for Letty. But since they've become official, he only seems to have treated her exactly as she deserves. And for that, I'm beyond grateful because of anyone I know, Letty deserves the happily ever after.

Having pity on her, I grab my still unopened notebook, shoving it into my bag, and then scoop up the shards of my now ruined pencil from the desk and slide out behind her. I drop the remains in the trash on the way out, looking at the pieces for a beat, seeing the resemblance to my life.

There's a massive crowd waiting for the elevator, so when Letty looks toward the stairs, I follow her lead, not wanting to be stuck in an enclosed space with a group of people right now.

I trail down behind her and then out into the winter sun. I squint against the brightness, feeling a little better getting some fresh air.

Nothing is said between us as we stand in line to order our coffees. Everyone else's stares and interest burn into me. The girls—the jersey chasers—blatantly strip me naked while the guys either stare at me with angry eyes for having that effect on their girls or for the fact I've lost them their season. Either is a valid reason, to be fair.

"Dunn," the server calls, her cheeks turning a deep crimson when I look at her and take my coffee.

"Thanks," I mutter, giving her zero special attention, but still she damn near pisses her pants.

Don't get me wrong, there are many, many times

where I've lapped up this kind of attention. The adoring fans, screaming crowds, girls who would sell their left tit to have a night with me. I'm a college guy, of course I've made the most of that over the years, who fucking wouldn't. But right now, I want them all to go away. I need the pity in their eyes to vanish and their attention to dwindle. I'd hoped it would after I lost us the championship, but now instead of everyone looking at me like they either want to be me or bang me, they're looking at me and wondering where it all went wrong. How their golden boy went from the epic high of last season to the pitiful low of this one.

I blow out a frustrated breath as I fall down into a chair that ensures I have my back to the rest of the coffee shop. I know they'll still be staring, but at least I don't have to watch them do it.

"It's still weird seeing you as such a celebrity," Letty says lightly, unable to miss the fact that the volume of the place dropped and all eyes turned on me from the second we entered.

I scoff, reaching out for one of the cupcakes she loves so much and pulling the wrapper off.

Taking a huge bite, I let the sweetness explode in my mouth in the hope it'll help sweeten my mood.

"What?" I mutter with a mouthful of cake when I pull it away.

"You really need to shave." Letty laughs, reaching over and wiping a generous blob of icing and sprinkles from the overly long scruff above my top lip.

I watch as she puts her finger in her mouth innocently to wipe it off. Not so long ago that move would have done things to me, but right now I feel nothing. But I don't think that's because I've accepted our reality and more just because I'm dead inside right now. The only thing that gets my blood pumping is the thought of torturing Peyton some more.

I shift in the chair as I think about Tuesday night once again before remembering that Letty said something.

"Y-yeah," I say, lifting my hand to my chin. "I know, I just..."

"Don't make excuses, Luc. I know you, remember." She pins me with a look that makes me feel about two inches tall.

"Let, I'm—"

"Don't," she snaps. "Don't apologize and assume everything is just going to go back to how it once was."

"It won't though, will it? You're with him."

"Luc," she breathes, looking up to the ceiling as if she needs some strength for this conversation.

"That wasn't what I meant. I get it, Let. Okay? I fucking get it." Pushing the rest of my cupcake away, I rest my elbows on the edge of the table and shove my fingers into my hair. "It was never meant to be us."

"You know, if it were four years ago then maybe it could have been."

Slowly, I lift my head and find her dark eyes.

"Oh come off it. As if you didn't know I had the biggest crush on you." She rolls her eyes at herself, embarrassment heating her cheeks and down her neck.

"You slept with Leon," I blurt, pain slicing through my heart as I remember that revelation.

"And you slept with half the female population of Rosewood High. It's all in the past, Luc. We did some stupid shit. I'm sure we'll continue to do stupid shit. But I want to do it knowing that you've got my back." Her expression softens and my frozen heart begins to melt a little.

"Does he really make you happy?"

"Yes, he does. He really does."

I nod at her, reaching for my coffee and pulling it closer.

"I know the two of you will probably never see eye to eye. But if you could at least try to tolerate each other, it would mean the world to me."

"I tolerate him just fine," I mutter, thinking of him being a much bigger part of my life than I ever wanted or expected him to be.

I thought exchanges with Kane Legend were done once I graduated. I thought he'd disappear into the pits of hell that was Harrow Creek, destined for a life of gangs, drugs, and crime. But no, apparently the universe had other ideas. As if I didn't already have enough to deal with.

Letty scoffs. "That's what you call tolerating?

You're gonna have to get used to it. You're not going to be getting rid of him next season."

"I know," I mutter. The truth of it is, while I might be worried about Letty being with him, I'm not stupid enough to deny that he needs to be standing beside Leon and me on the Panther's offense. Unfortunately, he's the best man for the job. While I might place the majority of last season's failing on my own shoulders, I can't lie and say that his name also doesn't feature seeing as he ended up on the bench injured more than he played. And as much as I might hate it, the three of us are a good team on the field. If we have any chance of making a comeback next season then we need to solidify them, and sadly, that means that we're going to have to spend some time together. Assuming I want to be back on the field next season.

Letty's cell bleeping cuts off whatever she was going to say and she pulls it from her back pocket, opening the message and almost instantly laughing to herself at whatever is on the screen.

"His cock that small, huh?" I ask, although I've probably seen that motherfucker naked as many times as she has, so I know it's not true. Asshole.

"Nah. Ella insisted on a toga fitting last night. There was a lot of tequila involved. Look." She turns her cell around and my eyes land on Ella and Violet, two of Letty's old roommates, dancing around in their dorm room wrapped in what looks like cut-up bedsheets.

They're laughing and joking, clearly totally

wasted but it's not the sight of them that makes my heart jump into my throat, because that's the flash of pink hair in the bottom left of the screen.

All the air rushes from my lungs but I quickly tell myself to get a grip. Loads of girls have pink hair on campus.

She's not even here. She spends too much time shaking her tits for assholes to attend classes.

But it was her night off, a little voice says in my head.

Shutting it all down, I look back to Letty as she takes her cell back.

"Looks like it was quite a night."

A genuine smile curls at her lips and I can't help but copy her. There were so many times she looked utterly miserable after she first started here last year, I love seeing her looking more like her fun-loving old self.

"Oh yeah, it was something. Those two were trashed."

The question about the pink haired girl is right on the tip of my tongue, but I swallow it down, not wanting to alert Letty to something—something that I'm sure is nothing more than me jumping to conclusions.

The two of them never met. Letty arrived only a few weeks after Peyton left, and although she's aware that my old friend left on bad terms, Peyton never came to visit, and even talking about her turned me into a dark, angry beast that I needed to keep hidden behind closed doors, and the best way to deal with that was to do my best to forget any of it even happened, that Peyton never even existed.

Letty's probably heard her name many times over the years, and now understanding just how close her and Leon were, it makes me wonder if she knows more than she ever let on. Not that Leon ever knew the whole truth. It was bad enough that I had to deal with Peyton's lies. I wasn't poisoning my brother's mind with them too.

"You're coming Friday night, right?" she asks after putting her cell away.

"Uh..." Honestly, I'd mostly planned to sit outside The Locker Room like a sad motherfucker and wait for my daily hit of Peyton.

I wrap my hand around the back of my neck, realizing just how fucking pathetic I'm becoming needing a look at a girl in the dead of night to settle the darkness within me.

"Oh come on. Everyone is over the season. You need to stop sulking and enjoy your free time before it starts all over again."

"I'm not sulking," I mutter, earning myself a raised eyebrow in return. "Okay. Fine. I'll be there."

We finish our coffees and chat about bullshit like classes and assignments, both of us skirting around the more serious topics that we've only touched on.

The two of us are going to need more than this little coffee ice breaker until we're back on some kind of level footing again.

When it's time for us to head to our next classes, I pull her in for a hug and hold her tight, breathing in her familiar and comforting scent as my heart aches once more and confusion clouds my brain.

"I'll see you soon, yeah?" she asks hesitantly as if she's about to walk away and it'll shatter the progress we've just made.

"Yeah. Maybe you and that guy of yours should even come and hang at the house sometime," I offer, although I'm not entirely sure if I mean it or not.

I walk away with a heavy heart, but the knowledge that I'm closer to seeing Peyton again puts a bit of a spring into my step as I walk toward my afternoon class.

9

PEYTON

I feel him the second I step out of the building, just like I did last night when my shift ended. But just like last night, he remains in the shadows, lurking, watching me, probably scheming up all the ways he can torture me.

I try to force myself to be scared, but I'm not. I might not be able to predict Luca's actions, the things he's thinking like I once could, but one thing has not changed. When I'm with him, I feel safe. Which is ironic because he should be the person I'm most terrified of right now.

Keeping my eyes focused on the dark corner of the lot, I move toward my car waiting for him to emerge. But he never does.

As I drop down into my driver's seat, I can't deny the disappointment that races down my spine. I shiver, my skin prickling with coldness that he's keeping his distance.

It's what I should want. But I don't.

At least if he's in front of me then I have half a chance of making him see the truth, of being able to convince him that I never once lied to him. That what I told him, although hard to hear and accept, was the truth.

I sigh, thinking of that sweet little boy hopefully tucked up in his bed at Aunt Fee's. He never asked for this. He doesn't deserve this. It's why I do this. I look up to the building, my fingers curling into fists. Tonight wasn't bad. It wasn't like Tuesday night, but still. It's not good. It's still not where I actually want to be.

With a long sigh, I start my car and pull out of the lot. I'm hardly surprised when headlights come on behind me and follow me out.

My heart jumps into my throat that he could be going to the same place as me. I didn't want to go to this party, but if he's going to be there, then... shit. Then it's exactly where I want to be.

"Shit," I hiss to myself as I turn down the street for the frat houses.

I glance in my mirror, expecting him to still be tailing me, but he's gone.

My heart sinks. Does he not care now I'm away from The Locker Room? What exactly is he waiting for, the opportunity for someone else to accost me like he did the other night?

The thought that he could be protecting me flickers through my mind. That's what the old Luca would have done but I squash the thought immediately because there's no way it's that.

He just wants to torture me, punish me. Prove that I'm nothing better than a filthy liar.

The knot in my stomach grows as I pull up somewhere close to where tonight's party is being held. The street is lined with cars and people all dressed similarly to how I should be.

All I've got to do is send one message and my little makeover team will appear to ensure I look the part.

Or I could make some excuse and head home to curl up in my bed.

"Argh," I scream when someone bangs on my car window, making me jump off the seat in fright. But when I look up, it's just a group of drunk guys enjoying their night.

They soon move on, leaving me in the solitude of my car but I know I can't sit out here all night, so I need to make a decision.

Pulling my cell from my purse, I send the message I need to and wait.

Not six minutes later do Ella and Letty come racing down the street. Letty looks relatively sober but Ella looks about as wrecked as she was on Wednesday night. This is not going to be good.

They both look like goddesses as they get closer. The pristine white sheet looks insane against Letty's bronzed skin and Ella's toga shows off every one of her wicked curves.

I feel completely inadequate as they descend on me.

Ella rips open my door and smiles down at me.

"Get in the back, girl," she slurs. "I need to work my magic."

Somewhat reluctantly, I climb from the seat.

"Here, you might need this," Letty says, handing me a small bottle of vodka.

"Thank you," I say, taking it from her.

She takes my seat, although sits backward so she can watch me get attacked by Ella in the back.

"Makeup," she demands and Letty throws my purse through the seats to her.

It's dark out so I have no clue how I'm going to look after this, but I go with it. Ella might be trashed but I trust Letty enough not to let me walk into the party looking like Frankenstein.

"Off," she demands, shoving the last of my makeup back into its bag.

I pull my tank off and shimmy out of my skirt.

"Off," she says again, looking down at my boobs.

"Umm..." Glancing over her shoulder, I take in the people that are still loitering out on the street.

"We've seen a pair of tits before, girl."

Reaching behind me, I unsnap the fabric. "It wasn't you two I was worried about."

"No one will see anything. I'll be like lightning."

I stare at her in the shadows now Letty has turned the interior light off so my naked breasts aren't like a homing beacon for horny college guys. She doesn't respond to the incredulous look on my face. She is way too far gone to do anything at the speed of light, other than falling face-first to the floor, I'm sure.

But much to my surprise, no sooner has my bra left my skin does the softness of the sheet wrap around me and I breathe a sigh of relief.

"I don't know what you're worried about, your tits are insane. If I swung the other way, I totally would." Ella winks.

"Oh my God," Letty groans with a laugh.

"What? She's got a great rack. Any guy would be lucky to have a pop on those babies."

"You need to be cut off," Letty tells her, reaching for the bottle Ella stashed amongst my discarded clothes.

"Nah, what I need is to get laid and that is certainly not going to happen while we're hiding in here. So come on, I'll pin the rest outside."

I look down at myself showing off way more skin than I was when we had our little fitting session the other night.

"Are you sure this is—"

"You look hot, now get out."

Unable to do anything but what I'm told, I slip my shoes on and slide out of the back of the car.

There are a few shouts and whistles as I emerge. I have no idea if it's a coincidence and I don't dare look up to find out.

Ella attacks the back of my toga, making me feel a little more secure in the thing now before running her fingers through my hair and making me twirl around to show them both the final look.

"Banging. Now let's go get drunk and dance the night away."

"Get drunk?" I mutter, much to Letty's amusement.

Ella throws my purse at me, allowing me to lock my car, and with them on either side of me, we head toward the house. To my first college party at MKU.

I'm sure it's a cookie-cutter duplicate of the ones back at Trinity, drunk college kids making memories that will embarrass them for the rest of their lives. There's only one difference here. I have no idea if Luca is inside this building or not. And if he's not here right now, he could turn up at any moment.

My heart tumbles in my chest and my steps falter as we get to the front door.

"Are you okay?" Letty asks.

"Y-yeah. That vodka hit me. I need food," I admit.

I went home between classes and work. Aunt Fee had made dinner but I could only pick at it, too anxious about what tonight was going to hold to really stomach any of it. But even though my nerves are completely shot right now, I know I need something before the alcohol hits me too hard and I make an even bigger mess of my life tonight.

At some point on the way to the kitchen, Ella disappears into the crowd but Letty makes sure I get there and deposits me by the mass of food that's been arranged on the kitchen island.

"Ah, a girl after my own heart," a familiar voice says as I reach for a handful of chips.

Looking over, I find one of the guys who lives in Ella and Violet's dorm. He's dressed in a toga—obviously—the loose fabric hanging from one shoulder and leaving very little to the imagination. If I didn't already know he was on the team then it wouldn't be hard to guess from looking at him.

It makes me wonder how well he knows Luca. If they're close. Was he one of the guys standing outside the coffee shop with him on Monday? Hell, I have no idea how well Ella or Letty know Luca.

"Hey, um..."

"Brax," he says.

"Y-yeah, of course."

"It's easy to remember. I'm the good-looking, smart one."

I chuckle at his idiocy. "I'll try to remember that."

"Our girl is looking hot, right?" Letty says, handing me a red Solo cup.

"Hell yes, shame I've already been warned off." His eyes drop down the length of me, lingering on the side boob that Ella left me with before finally meeting my eyes.

"Ah look, the ugly, dense one," I deadpan as West joins us making both Brax and Letty choke on their recently sipped drinks.

"Uh... got an issue, new girl?" he asks, although there's no malice behind his words.

"No. Brax here was just telling me that I can tell

him apart from you because he's the good-looking, smart one."

"Is that right?" he asks, turning to his friend.

"Only telling the lady the truth." Brax shrugs.

"I'm banging your girl tonight."

"I don't have a girl."

"Nope because your cock is so small that no one wants to bounce on it. But whoever you end up dancing with, she's mine, motherfucker. I'll show her how a real man does it."

"Fuck you, man. You've only got all of that on display in the hopes of distracting them from the reality under your toga."

"Oookay. As fun as this little cock measuring contest is," Letty says lightly. "We've got places to be."

With her arm around my shoulders, she leads me away from the guys and out of the kitchen. The music gets louder as we weave together through the crowds and toward the back of the house.

"Oh wow," I breathe, taking in the floor-to-ceiling windows that showcase the twinkling lights and pool in the garden.

"Yeah, the Kappas have a pretty sweet thing going on," Letty says beside me. "There's El and Vi, come on." She nods to the crowd but I have no chance of seeing them with all the people grinding it up on the makeshift dance floor. I do, however, look around for someone else, but I don't see him anywhere.

Plastering a smile on my face, I follow Letty through the crowd and lose myself to the music pounding through the speakers almost the second we join the other two.

"Your man not here tonight?" I shout to Letty. I was kind of hoping to meet this enigma of a man who's stolen her heart.

"Yeah, he is," she calls back. "He's with some friends. I'm sure he'll find me before too long."

And she's not wrong because not two songs later does the crowd before us part and a hot but slightly terrifying guy marches straight up to Letty, wraps his hand around her throat and slams his lips down on hers.

Whoa.

My temperature spikes just watching them as he crushes her slender body against his and totally consumes her.

I'm immediately taken back to having Luca squashing me between his hard body and his car. How would that have felt if it were fueled by desire, not hate and vengeance.

"You get used to them eventually. Just be glad you never experienced living in a dorm with them," Ella shouts in my ear as she rests her arms over my shoulders, encouraging me to dance with her.

"That good, huh?"

"My batteries died."

I bark out a laugh as we're joined by the other guys. Brax steps up behind Ella, his eyes flicking between the two of us rolling our hips to the music.

"Now this is something I can get on board with," he announces happily.

"Shut up, you dog," Ella snaps, but with a wink, she turns her back on me and begins dancing with him. He whispers something in her ear and she throws her head back with a laugh.

Jealousy washes through me at their easy relationship. West has Violet in his arms, the two of them enjoying themselves in the same relaxed manner.

My heart sinks as I think of years gone by when I'd have got that same comfort and enjoyment from dancing with Luc.

"Dance with me?" a voice says over my shoulder.

Spinning, I find their final dorm member. Only, he hardly resembles the guy I met briefly on Wednesday night as he ripped into the other two. His geeky glasses are gone and his hair has been styled away from his face. He looks... hot. And the fact I know that he's not a part of the team—or at least I assumed he's not seeing as he looked more nerd than jock the other night—means I'm even more drawn to him.

With a smile, I hold my hand out to him. "I'd love to."

Drinks are delivered to us courtesy of a few of the freshman team members and after being assured that they're totally trustworthy by everyone, I happily knock each one back until all my limbs begin to feel heavy and my head starts to swim.

It's the best I've felt in a long time as I move my body against Micah, a wide smile splitting my face as we all enjoy ourselves and just for a few hours, I'm able to let go.

Coming here was the right decision tonight. I have no idea what I was even so worried about.

"W e didn't think you were coming," Colt says when I join him and a few of the guys in the backyard.

"Here." Evan passes me a beer. "Glad to see you made an effort," he mutters, glancing down at my hoodie, Panthers jersey, and dark jeans.

I might have shown up but like fuck was I going to the effort to wrap myself in a fucking toga. In years gone by, yes, I was all over that shit. But right now? Nah. I'm here for the beer and hopefully the pussy, assuming I can get someone else out of my head for long enough to perform that is.

The memory of her looking right at me tonight despite the fact I know she couldn't actually see me hits me, and my cock swells.

What would have happened if I got out and walked toward her? Would she have run, or would she continue to play this little cat-and-mouse game we've got going on? Something tells me that it would be the latter. My cock twitches once more. I really fucking hope it would be the latter.

"Whatever," I grumble, lifting the bottle to my lips and draining half of it down in one.

"Been anywhere nice?" Leon asks, emerging from the crowd dressed like every other motherfucker here.

"You know, here and there."

"Riiight. Few more of them and maybe I'll get you to confess."

"It's none of your damn business," I snap.

It doesn't escape my attention that while I let Letty off pretty easily the other day, I'm still very much holding a grudge with Leon. What he did, the fact he's lied to me about it for so many years when I didn't think we kept shit like that from each other hurts.

You haven't told him about Peyton, a little voice screams in my head.

Lifting the bottle once more, I try to drown my conscience out. Knowing that he can easily keep stuff from me makes it easier to do.

He shakes his head at me. "Fine. You do your thing. But don't come running to me when it blows up in your face." Turning his back on me, he walks up to a couple of jersey chasers, accepting a drink from one of them and knocking it back like he doesn't care.

It's all a lie though. I can tell by the hard set of his

shoulders that he does. He cares more than he'll ever admit.

There's only one person I know who's able to hide the truth about what's really going on with them better than me, and that's my twin brother.

I know almost everything about him. But there's something, something buried deep that he keeps locked up tight, I just know there is.

I used to think it was just teenage hormone bullshit, but as we get older, that darkness in his eyes never seems to vanish.

No one else sees it. They all see the slightly moody, colder version of the playboy act I put on. But I see it and I've ignored it for years in the hope that one day he'd confess to whatever it was but I'm starting to think that whatever it is, he's going to take to his grave.

He has every right to do that, even if it does piss me off beyond belief.

Lifting my hand, I drag my hair back, wondering if I should just come clean to him. Tell him everything that happened back then. I remember feeding him with some bullshit about her cheating on me and then her mom getting a better job in South Carolina, severing all our ties.

He bought it, or I think he did, because he never really questioned it.

How would he react if he knew what really went down, if he heard the lies that spewed from her lips?

A commotion from the back doors finally pulls

my eyes from the dark, starlit sky above me and the house.

A group of drunk students all go down like dominoes as they try to get out of the house, and while on another day it might amuse me, right now I barely give them all a second glance because something catches my eyes through the glass door.

Pink. I saw pink.

Placing the bottle on the table beside me, I snatch up a new one and take a step forward.

No. It can't be.

It's just the random girl from Letty's video.

It can't be.

I take another step forward but whoever it is has been swallowed by the crowd that's gathered on the makeshift dance floor.

But then it parts once more and this time, I'm in the perfect line of sight.

The bottle falls from my hand as I watch her dancing with Micah at her back and none other than Letty at her front, who is of course attached to Kane fucking Legend.

Glass shatters at my feet, beer soaking my jeans as people surround her once more and she vanishes almost as if she was never there in the first place.

But she was. I know she was.

"What the fuck, Dunn?" one of the Kappas barks when he sees the mess I march away from.

"Sorry, bro. I'll get one of my boys to clean it," I

promise, storming past him and straight inside without a second thought.

More than a handful of people try to talk to me as I make my way through the throngs of people, but as seems to be becoming normal since our failed season, most give me a wide berth while shooting me concerned looks. I get it, I know I'm kinda volatile since everything went to shit.

I stand in the doorway of the room where she is, resting my hip against the doorframe and just wait as I try to come up with a plan that isn't to publicly drag her out of here kicking and screaming so I can dump her back wherever it is she's crawled out from all of sudden.

But as angry as I am at seeing her here, in the middle of my life, with my fucking friends, I know I can't just storm in there. The last thing I need is the rest of them on my case.

I stand there with my heart thundering in my chest and my nails digging into my palms just waiting for the perfect time to make my move.

Does she know I'm here? And if she does, what exactly is she expecting me to do?

No one speaks to me, and I know why. Fury surrounds me like a dark storm cloud, lightning just waiting for the perfect time to strike.

"Luca, are you—" Zayn cuts off whatever he was about to ask me when my eyes meet his. "Whoa, okay. Maybe later." He backs away with his hands up in defeat before disappearing around the corner.

When I look back to Peyton, Micah has fucked off, leaving me the perfect opening to take his place.

Her back is completely bare, making my semi only get harder as I imagine what little she's wearing under that sheet. Whoever wrapped her in it did a good job of making her look like the filthy slut that she is.

My hands tremble with restraint by the time I come to a stop behind her.

Her scent floods my senses, making my mouth water as the bare skin of her back burns my front through my shirt.

She freezes before me as if without looking that she knows it's me.

"Who's your new friend?" I ask innocently, sliding my hand in the back of her hair and tugging until she has no choice but to look up at me.

"Luc, this is Peyton. Peyton meet Luca, Panther's captain, lady killer, douchebag extraordinaire."

"Hey," I complain, ripping my eyes from Peyton's narrowed ones to look at Ella who's thankfully stopped running her mouth. "What did I ever do to you?"

"Aside from not showing me heaven."

"Ignore her," Letty shouts over the music. "She's wasted. Makes her mouth a little easy."

"From what I hear, it's not just her mouth. Might want to watch that one, bro," I say to Brax, who's grinding up against her. "You have no idea where she's been."

"Fuck you, Luc," Ella hisses but sways on her feet, showing just how drunk she is.

"How did you miss the dress code for tonight?" Letty asks while Kane stares daggers at me and Peyton squirms against my hold.

I move against her with the music, my hand on her waist ensuring she rolls her hips with me, rubbing her ass against my quickly growing cock.

"Yeah, I must have missed that."

"Do you two know each other?" Kane asks, clearly not missing Peyton's reaction to me.

"Nope. But I've got a feeling we're about to. What do you say, Pink? Wanna come get a drink with me?"

My fingers both twist in her hair and dig into her waist ensuring only one answer falls from her lips.

"A drink with the famous QB1 of the Panthers. How could a girl say no?" she purrs sweetly. So much so, it's almost believable.

"Don't expect her back." I wink at Kane while Letty tenses in his hold. She probably thinks I'm doing this to teach her a lesson for being with him, but that's far from the truth. Letty isn't even on my radar right now. "Let's go," I growl in Peyton's ear, releasing her hair and steering her out of the room.

I swing by the kitchen for a bottle of vodka and thankfully, we bump into Owen, the Kappa president.

"Dunn, did you forget something?" he asks, taking in my clothes.

"Nope, I've got it right here. Listen, I need a

favor." I lean into his ear, whispering my request so that Peyton can't hear.

He nods and in seconds pulls a key from somewhere in his toga. I wrap my fingers around it, trying to ignore the fact it's warm.

"Enjoy, man. And if you make a mess, clean it the fuck up."

"You got it, man. Later."

He nods at me, and with my hand still locked around Peyton's waist, I direct her outside and around the side of the impressive building, ensuring we go in the opposite direction of where I last saw Leon and head toward the pool house.

"Luca, what the hell are you doing?" she hisses, but at no point does she try to escape me. I tell myself that it's because she wants to be with me and not just because she doesn't want to make a scene in front of a massive portion of MKU.

"Shut up," I snap. "You don't need to talk."

All the air rushes from her as a disgruntled noise rips from her throat.

My grip tightens on her waist, my finger digging into her soft skin enough to leave marks.

The thought of her waking up in the morning with the evidence that I was this close to her is the final straw and by the time I push the key into the lock, my cock is trying to bust out of my jeans. Fucking good thing I'm not wearing a bedsheet right now.

"Get the fuck in," I say, pushing Peyton inside

with my hand on the nape of her neck. She stumbles on her heels and falls into the couch as I once again lock the doors and pocket the key to stop her escape.

"I will ask you this once," I say, although it pains me to do so. "Do you want an audience for what's about to go down or would you prefer to keep it just between us?" I run my eyes down her barely covered body. Her chest is heaving, the fabric of her makeshift dress just about keeping her tits concealed, the skirt high enough that I can see her white lace panties beneath.

Her eyes drill into me as her nostrils flare and her lips purse in anger.

"So? I have no problem with everyone out there knowing what a filthy slut you are."

My body trembles with adrenaline, fear, and dare I say it... desire.

He stares at me with dark eyes, the muscle in his neck is pulsating and his hands balled into tight fists.

Pushing up from the couch so I'm sitting, I keep my eyes locked on his, trying not to wither under the heat of his stare.

I have no idea what's running through his head right now, but none of it is good. My stomach clenches at the thought of a repeat of Tuesday night only... alone.

My heart rate picks up even more, making my already alcohol-buzzed head spin faster.

I shouldn't want this. I shouldn't be excited about being locked in a building with this man—this stranger. Because that's what he is. The boy I once used to know and love is long gone. The man standing before me is someone else entirely. He's angry, dangerous, and lethal. Three things I didn't know I wanted but hell if I can deny that I'm not just a little bit turned on right now.

"You have three seconds to answer or the entire college is going to be witness to me ruining you right there on the couch."

"C-close t-them," I stutter, knowing that I need this to be between just us.

This isn't about anyone else. It's not about the people involved in ruining us. It's just us exorcising some demons. I just only hope that we can move past them once this is done.

He doesn't move and just as I start to think it was a trick question, that he was going to allow everyone to witness what happens next, he finally turns around.

The blinds are twisted closed and immediately it feels like the room has halved in size.

I fight to drag in the air I need but the second the air hits my nose, all I smell is him.

"Luc, what are you—"

"Why, P? Why are you here?"

I hesitate for a second but when I do try to answer he doesn't allow me. "Because I—"

"You're at MKU, aren't you?" he barks, his jaw popping with restraint.

"Yes," I confess although my voice is so quiet I doubt he actually hears it. He doesn't need to. He already knows the answer.

"Why? Why would you come here knowing that I was here? And don't try to play the innocent, P. I know you're not stupid enough to not know where I am."

"I knew you were here. I've watched your games."

All the air rushes from his lungs at my words.

"Y-you watch—fuck. FUCK," he bellows, his fingers tugging at his hair until it has to hurt.

I stare at him wondering if I'm about to watch him shatter. Scooting forward, I'm just about to push to stand when he lifts his eyes from the floor and locks them on mine.

A shiver races down my spine at the warning I can read within them.

"Luc?" I whisper but I think he's too far gone to hear anything right now.

He's before me in a heartbeat, his long, powerful legs eating up the distance faster than I thought possible.

His burning hot fingers wrap around my throat and squeeze enough to warn me of just how strong he is but without actually hurting me.

My ass leaves the couch until I'm standing in front of him.

"You don't belong here."

His eyes are so dark as he stares into mine that they're almost black, but even still, I can't find it in me to actually be scared of him.

"I-I didn't have a choic—argh," my squeal of surprise as he surges me backward cuts off my words. An umph falls from my lips as my back hits the wall.

He crowds me against the wall, his wide chest heaving with his anger, his scent utterly consuming me and the heat from his body turning my blood to lava.

"You. Do. Not. Belong. Here," he spits.

"So what are you going to do about it?"

A gasp rips from my throat as he reaches out and tugs at the fabric wrapped around me. It falls away as if it's no more than tissue leaving me once again exposed to him. Only this time, we're standing under fluorescent lighting and he can see everything. There's no hiding in the shadows right now.

Unable to look at him as he stares down at my breasts, I focus on a spot on the floor as my cheeks burn with embarrassment. It might not be the first time he's seen me naked, but that was years ago, my body has changed since then. We were still kids when we started experimenting with each other, now we're adults.

My nipples harden to the point of pain as his attention continues to burn into them. My breathing is erratic, giving away just how I'm feeling right now.

I wish I could be indifferent to his undivided attention but I can't. It's always been the same between us. I was always super aware of him, but as we became teenagers and my hormones started to kick in, I was acutely aware if he was in the room, if he was looking at me. For a long time, I didn't understand it. But I do now. I'd just hoped it might have fizzled out with our time apart.

"Look at you," he says, his eyes finally lifting to my face once more, but I still keep my eyes on a knot in the wooden floor beneath us. "Practically begging for it. Is that what you're like at the bar? Begging for any bit of attention those men give you."

I bite down on the inside of my lips, not wanting to have to plead my innocence once more.

"Look at me, P."

I suck in a deep breath before lifting my eyes from the floor. I gasp when I see the darkness in his eyes.

"Do they get your nipples this hard? Make your chest redden with desire?"

I shake my head, unable to find any words even if I wanted to.

"You love knowing that you're turning them on, don't you? You love that your little innocent look gets them all hard for you. So why don't you try telling me again how you don't let them touch you, because from what I see, you're fucking begging for it."

"T-they don't—I don't—"

"Bullshit." He says the word so low that it almost sounds like a purr. The sound of it does delicious things between my thighs.

Damn him. Fucking damn him.

"At least I get to benefit from all the practice you've had," he mutters, his eyes full of wicked intent.

"Wha—" His hands land on my shoulders and I have no choice but to allow my knees to buckle.

"That's it, P. Get down there where you belong."

"Luc," I whimper but the sight of the bulge in his pants causes heat to flood my core.

"Too late to try and get out of this, P. You're already on your knees."

I watch, utterly captivated as he undoes his belt, pops the button, and lowers the zipper.

My mouth waters with anticipation and I stuff down the realization that I should not be turned on by this in the slightest.

This is Luc. Neither of us were ever very good at following the rules. That's exactly how we ended up in this position the very first time it happened when he snuck into my bedroom after Mom had gone to bed one night.

Without hesitation, he hooks his thumbs into the waistband of both his pants and boxers and pushes them over his hips.

His solid length springs free and my entire body tenses as I take it in.

Fuck, he's bigger than I remember.

When I don't move, only stare at the angry purple head that's already got a bead of precum glistening at the tip, he wraps his fingers around himself.

Ripping my eyes from the sight of him pleasuring himself, I move them up his shirt, wishing it was gone and I could get a look at what he's hiding beneath. Finally, I find his eyes as he glares down at me.

"Problem?" he asks, lifting a brow, his hand still moving up and down his shaft.

"Um..." I suck my bottom lip into my mouth, the thought of tasting him again is almost too much to deny but hell if I want to look like I want this.

His eyes lock on my lips and I bite down on the bottom one causing a growl to rumble at the back of his throat.

The second I release my lip, his restraint snaps.

Threading his fingers painfully into my hair, he moves me exactly where he wants me before pushing his steel length past my lips.

He's not gentle, not like the boy I remember who never wanted to hurt me, instead, he surges forward until the tip of his cock hits the back of my throat and I can't help but gag at the intrusion.

"Much fucking better," he says, pulling out a little to allow me to drag in a breath. "You look right at home down there, P."

Before I'm ready, he thrusts forward again.

His taste, his size, his angry thrusts are the only things I can think about as he continues to fuck my mouth.

My lungs burn with my need for air and my eyes water as I gag around him, but he doesn't let up.

"Fuck, you look beautiful, baby."

That one word sends a shudder through the length of my body. It's said so much softer than anything else he's spat at me tonight and it makes me think of the boy I used to know.

Is he still in there buried beneath the anger?

Saliva drips from my chin as his cock swells even bigger and his grip on my hair becomes unbearable, as if he's about to rip it clean from my scalp.

Just when I don't think I can take anymore, his cock jerks violently in my mouth before he shoots hot jets of cum down my throat. He holds himself deep as he finishes, his loud groan of pleasure echoing off the walls of the pool house.

The second he's done, he pulls out of my mouth and leans down, wrapping his hand around my throat once more and pulling me to my feet.

I just about manage to wipe the drool from my chin before his dark stare renders me useless.

"Not bad," he growls. "Took the edge off at least." His eyes flick down to my bare chest once more.

The tension crackles between us as his eyes flick between mine and my lips.

Surely he's not going to kiss me after that.

"Great. Can I go now?" I ask. I know I'm pushing my luck and if I'm being honest with myself, I'll be disappointed if he says yes and lets me walk out before discovering exactly what he has planned for me.

In a move I wasn't expecting, a smile twitches at his lips before it splits right across his face. It's the most beautiful sight, even with the anger still darkening his green eyes.

"Can you go now?" he repeats before laughing. It's so light and happy that anyone overhearing might think I'd just told him a joke, although I think to him, I just did. "Sure," he says, taking a giant step back. His eyes remain on mine as he tucks himself away, but he never does his fly up as he continues to back away. "You can walk out of here right now if you plan on leaving town, taking your lying, filthy mouth with you, and never show your face again."

My lips part to argue, to tell him that I can't do that but it seems I don't need to.

"But you won't, will you? You've got a loving boyfriend waiting for you at home. That is who I saw welcome you back the other night with open arms, right? Where is he now, huh? Do you think he has any idea that you've just had my cock in your mouth? Do you think he'd be happy to know that you put up zero fight about it?"

I want to tell him that Elijah isn't my boyfriend but I have a feeling that even if I tried, he wouldn't listen to me. He only wants to believe what he wants. That I'm a liar and a cheat. The reality is that I'm neither.

"I'm not leaving town, Luc. And not because of him."

"No? Because of who then... me?" he spits.

"Oh yeah, because you've been so warm and welcoming," I deadpan, wrapping my fingers around the bedsheet hanging at my waist, ready to cover myself up. I barely lift the fabric before he notices.

"Strip."

"What."

"You heard me."

"But I just..." I look down at his crotch indicating what I just did and he laughs.

"You think that was it? You think all of this is all over because you gave me one half-decent blowjob?"

My chin drops but I don't have any words.

He walks back until his legs hit the edge of the couch, then he drops down, swiping the vodka he brought in with us from the coffee table and twisting the top. He spreads his legs wide and tips the bottle to his lips, swallowing down a generous amount and ensuring I focus on the muscles in his throat rippling as he does.

"Now," he says, finding my eyes once more. "Strip."

"Luc, this is insane," I try to argue.

"Okay," he says, getting comfortable for the show. "Then tell me the truth. Tell me that you're a lying cunt and apologize for what happened."

My teeth grind at his demand because he knows full well that I'm not going to do that.

"I didn't lie, Luc," I hiss, although I don't know why I bother because if he didn't believe me then, why would he now? The only way to prove it is to... no. I refuse to even consider the option. Luca hating me, torturing me, is better than allowing him into my life and revealing the truth.

It'll hurt him, sure. But he's not my biggest

concern anymore. There's someone else who's more important who doesn't need his world to be flipped over once again.

He stares at me, his face void of emotion. Reaching into his pocket, he pulls out his cell and after a second, the sexy beat of a Rhianna song fills the space.

Lifting the bottle, he tips it toward me. "Go on then. Show me how you earn your money."

"I'm not a fucking stripper, Luc."

He quirks a brow.

"Or a hooker," I add, knowing exactly what he's thinking.

"No, you just walk around with your nipples out for any asshole who cares to look. Your boyfriend must really fucking love you to allow you to do that. If you were mi—" He cuts himself off, preferring to drown the unspoken words in vodka instead of letting them hang between us.

"Yours?" I ask with a laugh. "If I were yours?"

His brows pull together as he studies me.

Every muscle in my body screams at me to cover up but I refuse to show even an ounce of weakness around him right now.

12

———

LUCA

"*If I were yours?*"

Her words repeat over and over in my head as she stands there trying to appear confident before me when I know that deep down, all she wants to do is cover up. Her nose twitches in a way that I used to think was utterly adorable. I'd put her in any awkward situation just to see that twitch.

YOU used to be mine. YOU fucked it up. YOU lied to me. YOU ruined us.

But still, I can't help wondering what the fuck her boyfriend is playing at allowing her to walk around looking like she does at The Locker Room.

Unless... what she's saying is true and he's not her boyfriend. She was just very willingly gagging on my cock.

Is she really a cheat as well as a liar?

I think back to her jumping into his arms only days ago. They certainly seemed close.

I lift the bottle to my lips once more, the vodka no longer burning as it goes down. But it's not doing a fucking good job of numbing everything I don't want to be feeling.

Grabbing my cell once more, I turn the volume up.

"I'm done waiting, P. I want action." I turn it louder to ensure she can't respond, or at least if she does, I can't hear it.

Pushing everything aside, our past, her possible boyfriend, the fact my heart beats that little bit faster than it should whenever I'm anywhere near her and the ache in my balls despite the fact I've only just come down her throat, I watch her.

She drops her hands to the rope around her waist, but she makes no move to undo it.

After a beat, I lean forward, resting my elbows on my knees and allowing the now half-empty bottle to hang between.

I stare at her as defiance flickers through her silver eyes.

"Peyton," I warn, knowing that she'll be able to hear it loud and clear despite the volume of the music.

She tilts her chin up and stares at me, her chest heaving and her nipples still hard, begging for attention.

Not touching them this far has damn near killed me.

I stand, killing the music in the process. Clearly, she's not going to make use of it, and I'm going to have to get involved then I want her to hear every single thing I'm going to growl in her ear.

"You're playing a dangerous game here, P," I warn.

"I can handle you, Luc."

"Nah," I say, taking another swig of vodka. "You handled me as a boy. You have no fucking clue what you're getting into with me now."

I don't need to be touching her to know a shudder just worked its way down her body.

"Open," I demand, holding the bottle up to her lips.

I pour some in, watching as it runs from the corners of her mouth and drops from her chin and onto her breasts.

Lifting my other hand, I run my fingertip through the stream of liquid.

"Luca," she breathes when I circle her nipple, making it pucker even more.

"You're so fucking desperate, P." I lean in close to whisper in her ear. "I can smell you. But I doubt you taste as sweet as you used to. Bitter and sour. I bet that's how you taste now after all your lies and bullshit."

She shakes her head.

"You can tell me the truth at any time, you know. I might even take pity on you and let you go." It's a barefaced lie, she's not walking through those doors for a very long time yet.

Her expression hardens and she once again lifts her chin slightly.

"Right choice, baby. I want to fuck the truth out of you too. I'm glad we're on the same page."

Her eyes hold mine and I can see the argument she's desperate to spit at me within them, but she never does.

Why? Why doesn't she just tell me everything?

Because she doesn't want to admit to being a liar.

"Luc," she cries as I twist her around and push her into the blinds. The wooden slats clatter against the glass as Peyton's breathing becomes erratic.

Filthy little bitch like this. My cock gets hard again just at the thought alone.

Pressing the length of my body against her back I breathe into her ear as my hands slip around her waist to the knot in the rope that's tied around her.

"Imagine how you'd look to my team right now if you didn't request I close the blinds." She swallows loudly. "They'd get to see your rosy, hard nipples pressed against the glass. They'd see the heat of your cheeks, the desire in your eyes."

"Luc," she whimpers.

"That turn you on, baby, imagining them watching you?"

Finally loosening the rope, I pull it from around her body.

"Would you want them to watch me as I fucked you too?" She trembles against me. "Or would you like them to join, is that it?"

"No," she cries.

"It could be arranged. It wouldn't be the first time we've tag-teamed. Did you have anyone in mind?"

She shakes her head violently as I run my knuckles down her arms causing goose bumps to erupt in their wake. She's like putty in my hands and fuck if it's not exactly as I've imagined for the best part of five years.

"Or maybe you want to try out the twin thing," I continue, distracting her with my wicked words as I wind the rope around her wrists. "Letty has been between us. Did you know that?"

"No. Luc, no. I don't want them."

"No? Who is it you want then?" I ask, running my lips around the shell of her ear, a smile pulling at my lips when she trembles again. "Lie to me again, baby. I dare you," I warn.

"Y-you, Luc. I want you."

"Right answer, baby. Although I still don't think you have any clue what you're asking for."

"I know what I want, Luca," she spits.

"And what if I don't want to give you what you want?"

She shrugs but pauses with her shoulders up as she must realize for the first time what I've done.

"Luc?"

"Well, well... look at that. You're totally at my mercy now, baby. What am I going to do with you?"

Finally finding the pin that's holding the fabric around her waist, I pull it out and watch in delight as the fabric finally falls away from her body.

"Whoops," I breathe innocently in her ear.

Sliding my hands around her waist and to her stomach, I pull her away from the window and into me.

"For someone who claims not to be a slut, you're not fighting very hard to stop this."

"Who said I wanted to stop it? Maybe I want your punishment, your torture, your cock."

Her words are like fuel to the already out-of-control fire that's burning red hot inside me.

"Filthy. Slut."

Skimming one hand up, I finally cup one of her heavy, needy breasts in my hand, pinching her nipple between my fingers.

Needing to know just how badly she wants what she just said, I push the other hand lower, my fingers dipping under her white lace panties.

Her pussy is smooth as I get lower.

"I bet those dirty old men love your smooth pussy."

She tenses in my hold but any response that she was going to bite back is cut off by a soft whimper then I part her and find her clit.

I push lower and find exactly what I was expecting.

"Oh baby," I moan, pushing two fingers inside her dripping center. "Did you like sucking my cock?"

"Luc," she moans, her hips rolling, riding my hand.

Ripping my hand from her panties, I wrap it around her throat and walk backward, pulling her with me.

"Oh God," she cries when I push her bare tits against the small glass table. Pinning her in place with my hand on the nape of her neck, I rip her panties from her body with the other.

"Don't move a fucking inch," I warn as I kick her legs wide and drop to my knees, unable to resist getting just a little taste of her.

Parting her, I take in her pretty, slick pussy.

She always was fucking perfect, and I hate that she only looks better five years later.

"Oh, P. Look how swollen your clit is. You really did like my cock, huh?"

She whimpers, giving me the response I really didn't need.

Leaning forward, I run my tongue up the length of her pussy, allowing her sweetness to explode on my tongue.

My mouth waters. The taste of getting my vengeance after all these years is really fucking sweet.

"Luc, fuck," she cries when I latch on to her clit and suck it hard into my mouth.

She's so fucking wet, her juices run down my

chin but I fucking lap it up, eating her until she's only a breath from her release. It's then I pull back and wipe my mouth with the back of my hand.

"No, Luc. No. No, not again. Please."

"Give me one good reason why you deserve any pleasure," I tell her, pushing to stand and once again shoving my pants down over my ass, exposing my rock-hard cock.

I stare at her pussy, imagining what she's going to look like stretched full of me. My cock jerks with its need to find out.

"Because I've never lied to you in my life," she shouts, her voice bordering on manic.

"Not good enough." Without warning, I thrust forward, filling her up in one quick move.

"Luca," she screams, her body locking up in shock.

"Don't come."

"What?" she cries as if I just said the most bizarre thing she's ever heard.

"You do not come." Reaching forward, I slide my fingers into her hair and pull her head back. "You got that?" She attempts to nod. "Good, because you won't like what happens if you defy me."

"It gets worse?" she sasses.

"Don't test me, baby. I'm no longer an innocent fifteen-year-old boy. You have no idea what I'm capable of or all of the things I told myself I'd do to you if I ever saw you again."

My body moves without instruction from my

brain as I thrust into her, chasing the release I so desperately need. It might have only been minutes ago that I blew a load in her mouth, but fuck, I need more.

I fear I need more than I'm ever going to be able to get when it comes to Peyton.

"Luca," she cries, her body surging forward, her feet leaving the floor with my forceful movements.

"I said." Thrust. "Don't." Thrust. "Come."

"Oh God," she cries, her fingers curling around the edge of the table, her grip so tight her knuckles turn white.

"Yesss," I hiss as my balls start to draw up. "For a slut, you've got a tight little cunt, baby."

"Argh," she grunts, her muscles tightening around me as if she's about to fall.

Not wanting to risk her getting what she wants, I pull out of her, flip her around and jack my cock until hot jets of cum coat her tits.

"Filthy fucking slut," I mutter as I rub the sticky mess into her skin.

She watches my movement, not saying a word as I mark her with my seed.

When I finally pull back, her eyes lift to mine. Her mask has dropped momentarily and it's the first time I see how she's really feeling.

Tears fill her eyes as she looks up at me. Her makeup is smeared everywhere, her hair a matted mess, and her skin red and patchy from her almost orgasm.

"I hate you," she hisses. "I thought—"

"That I'd forget all about it? I thought you knew me better than that, baby." Reaching behind me, I pull my jersey over my head, but if she thinks I'm going to pass it over to her so she can clean up, she's going to be bitterly disappointed. Instead, I throw it toward the bedroom and swipe up my bottle of vodka.

I take a swig while her eyes track my every movement. I hate the way she studies me, as if she knows me, as if she can see past the act, the bravado and see the broken, hurt little boy who's still hiding beneath it all.

"Can I?" she asks, holding her hand out.

I stare at it for a beat, considering if I'm willing to share. But one glance at her spunk-covered tits and I pass it over.

We're so far from done right now, something tells me that she's going to need it.

"Thank you," she whispers, lifting it to her once red lips, swallowing down shot after shot.

Reaching up, I run my fingers through my hair, tracking my eyes down the smooth column of her neck, over the swell of her breasts and the indent of her waist.

Fuck, she's beautiful.

"What?" she barks, her eyes narrowing in frustration.

"Just taking in the changes."

"The biggest ones are on the inside," she confesses.

"Fucking tell me about it."

Swiping the bottle back, I drain the remaining vodka.

"So now what?"

Turning my back on her, I find where she abandoned her purse when I first locked us in here.

"Hey," she complains when I start rummaging through looking for her cell.

Holding it before me, I wake it up and find a message.

Letty: Are you okay? Do you need me to come and rescue you?

Irritation once again surges through me that Letty thinks that Peyton needs rescuing from me. I mean, she quite possibly might, but I didn't think Letty would think I was capable of hurting her. But then I guess after the state I've seen her in after some of her wilder rendezvous with Kane, I guess it just proves that maybe we didn't know each other all that well in the first place.

"Aw, how sweet. Letty wants to protect you from the big bad wolf," I say, holding up her screen so she can see it.

"You know her? Them?"

"Aw, baby. Letty was your replacement when you fucked off. She rolled into town right on cue."

"B-but she's engaged." Peyton's brow wrinkles in confusion.

"So she is. And you've got a boyfriend. Passcode?" I demand, not willing to go any farther down the Letty route because although what I just said was the truth, Letty didn't replace Peyton. No one could ever have done that back then. Hell, I'm not sure anyone could do it now either, but fuck if I'm confessing to that anytime soon.

Peyton stares at me, defiance shining bright in her eyes, but eventually she mumbles out four numbers that rattle my resolve.

They're the numbers we used to use for everything as kids. Our two birth dates.

My breathing catches but I force myself to rip my eyes away from hers and type it into the cell as if I haven't even noticed.

Opening her messages, I find the unread one from Letty at the top. The second one though, is from him. Although the name makes me pause for a beat.

Elijah. I know that name.

Elijah: Have a great night, you deserve it x

Pushing the nagging feeling that something isn't right here aside, I allow my anger to take over.

"Aw, isn't that sweet? He wants you to have a nice night. I wonder if he has any idea just what his little slut is getting up to. That she's standing naked before me right now with my jizz running down her tits."

Her teeth grind as she wraps her arms around herself, trying to hide from me.

She's going to need to try harder than that.

"What are you doing?" she hisses.

"Me?" I ask innocently. "Nothing. You, however, are going to tell Letty that you're fine, that I took you home when you got a little too drunk. You're also going to tell loverboy that you've decided to hang out with your friends this weekend instead of returning to suck his tiny cock." My thumbs fly over the screen as I explain exactly what I'm doing.

"He won't believe me."

"Well then, let him come looking."

The second I'm done, I turn her cell off and tuck it into my pocket.

"You made a mistake letting me lead you in here, P."

"Oh." She tilts her chin, trying to appear as if she has some kind of control over what's going to happen within these walls.

I chuckle, pushing my hair back and running my eyes down her insane curves. Yeah, she's different from what's been in my mind all this time. She's fucking better.

Marching up to her, I pull her into my body, pinning her there with a tight grip on the nape of her neck.

"You're not leaving this place until every single inch of your body knows who owns it."

"You had me, Luc, and you threw me away. I'll

never belong to you again." Her body trembles as she says the words, making me wonder just how forced they are. Something tells me that Peyton is very much aware of who she really belongs to. I'm more than happy to give her the evidence she needs.

"Yeah, we'll see about that, baby."

13

PEYTON

I'm thrown down on the bed, bouncing
unceremoniously in the center as Luca turns
his back on me and storms through a door off to
the side, the bathroom, I assume.

Not two minutes later does an ice cold cloth slap
down on my outstretched thigh.

"Clean yourself up, you look like a whore," he
barks before leaving the room.

I wince as I press the cloth to my chest, wiping
away the evidence of what he did. I try to clear the
memory of him marking me in such a primal way out
of my head as well, but that doesn't disappear quite as
easily.

Looking around the room, I try to find something
to cover up with. The closet calls to me, but a loud
crash from inside the small pool house startles me
and stops me from moving.

In the end, I settle for slipping under the covers. I

have no idea whose bed this is but right now I really don't care. With Luca gone, my body temperature is dropping by the second.

The clock on the nightstand ticks by but he doesn't return. I know he's still here though. I can sense him.

If he's trying to drive me crazy, then I hate to admit that it's working.

I rub my thighs together as I sit with the covers pulled up to my chest. My need to finish myself off is almost unignorable, but something tells me it would be a really stupid move to do something about it.

After long agonizing minutes, footsteps begin to get louder before his shadow fills the doorway.

Thanks to the drinks I've had tonight, plus the shots of vodka, my vision swims when I look at him.

Shirtless, the ink now covering one of his arms is clear to see, his pants are still undone at the waist, his hair is a mess and his face is still set as an emotionless mask. But that's not the most shocking thing, because that is the joint he's holding to his lips.

I hate it. This isn't the Luca I fell in love with all those years ago. This Luca is cold, cruel, vicious. His need to hurt me, to punish me for something that was entirely out of our control is the only thing he can see right now.

I know that I could probably make it better, that I could explain everything that happened since Mom dragged both me and Libby away to start new lives away from the lies.

Maybe if we'd stayed and she'd fought for what was right, then everything would have been different. The truth would have been exposed. My stomach twists, bile burning up my throat as I consider how many other young lives have been tainted because Mom decided to protect her own and keep the truth from the media.

"Luc, what are you doing?" I ask, my concern for my old friend taking precedence over my anger right now. Luca doesn't do drugs. His career is too important to him. So to see him standing there with a stream of smoke billowing from his lips is shocking.

He takes another deep drag before slowly releasing the smoke from one side of his mouth.

"Football," I breathe.

"It's cute that you care. Admirable, I guess."

He pushes from the doorframe and walks around the bed, his eyes holding mine.

"You covered up," he states.

"I was cold."

"Hmm..." rumbles up his throat.

Reaching forward, he pulls the sheets with one harsh tug. His strength is no match for mine and the fabric slips out of my grip and away from my body.

Curling up into a ball, my skin pricks with goose bumps as Luca digs his hand into his pocket and pulls out his cell.

"L-Luc, what are you d-doing?" I ask, my voice cracking with a mixture of emotion, exhaustion and frustration.

He keeps the camera trained on me as he takes a step closer.

"Getting some evidence."

"Evidence for what? To prove you tortured me and got your vengeance at last?"

"Something like that," he mutters.

Reaching out, his hot fingers wrap around my ankle and he pulls until I unfold and fall onto my back.

Mortification burns through me as he runs the camera over my naked body.

Part of me wants to believe that the Luca I knew and loved wouldn't do this to me. But I fear he might be long gone and that this new, evil version of himself wouldn't bat an eyelid about making this video and then sending it out to the world.

"P-please don't. Please," I beg, hating the desperation in my voice.

"Why? Don't you want the whole world to know that you're a filthy slut just like the rest of your family?"

I shake my head, trying to keep his words out.

"You know the guys at school used to jerk off to videos of your mom dancing, right?"

"No," I cry. But it's futile because I remember all too well the gossip that used to go around about her. My only saving grace back then was Luca because if anyone was stupid enough to say anything out of line in front of him, he'd deal with it. Protecting me. Always protecting me.

"And your whore of a sister. Guys used to pay her to blow them in the locker room, did you know that?"

"Luc, please," I try again, needing not to go down these painful parts of my past right now.

"You knew this. You knew what she was up to. I'm surprised you weren't as well. We all knew what the Banks girls did to keep a roof over their heads. But then I guess, that's exactly what you're doing now, isn't it? Following in mommy's footsteps and shaking these pretty little tits for money." He scoffs, lifting another bottle from his side that I didn't notice before and swallowing an obscene amount. "You disgust me."

"Didn't stop you fucking me bare out there though, did it," I point out, knowing for a fact that he didn't stop for a second to consider protection.

His entire body tenses at my words and I can't help the satisfied smirk that curls at my lips.

My core throbs as he stares at my closed thighs.

"I'll get tested tomorrow. I wouldn't believe you even if you said you were clean."

"Fuck you, Luc," I say, scrambling to my feet and standing before him, for once in my life having a height advantage. "I'm fucking clean *and* on birth control. You're safe."

He scoffs once more, downing more vodka.

"Safe. With you. Never."

His solid arm hooks around the back of my legs and the world falls out from beneath me as I hurtle toward the mattress once more.

No sooner than my back hitting the softness of

the mattress is he crawling between my thighs, pushing them wide and exposing every inch of me.

Somehow, he managed to shed his remaining clothes while I was flying through the air and my concern about my position melts away as I get my first look at him as a whole in five years.

And fuck, he's... he's... mesmerizing.

His hand wraps around my throat, pinning me to the bed.

Our eyes lock and for just a second, everything is different. Everything is just as it used to be as I stare into the hungry green eyes of my best friend.

But then he speaks, and I crash back down to reality with a violent bang.

"The only safe bet here is that your cunt is going to be obliterated by the time I allow you to hobble out of here. But—" he quickly adds. "Only one of us will have enjoyed it."

He thrusts inside me once more, clearly either believing that I'm clean or serious about just getting tested tomorrow. The thought of the latter makes my stomach turn. That he really thinks I'm that deceitful but the feeling of his length stretching me open soon consumes my every thought. It burns after his rough treatment over the table along with the fact it's not been used by anything that doesn't vibrate in... well... a really long fucking time. And because of that, I'm racing toward a release I already know I won't be allowed to ride out all too soon.

Pain slices through my body when I come to the next morning. I roll onto my back and just about to smother my moan as my muscles pull.

Memories of the reason for my aching body slam into me like a freaking movie. The dining table, the bed, against the wall, over the dresser, the shower.

"Fucking hell, Peyton," I chastise myself as I regretfully rip my eyes open against the harsh morning sunlight.

I blink as my eyes fill with water before looking to the other side of the bed. I already know what I'm going to find, I can feel his distance.

The sheets are a mess and there's a dent in the pillow, indicating toward the fact he was here at one point in the night. But he obviously didn't deem me a suitable sleeping partner because he's left me alone.

Sucking in a deep breath, I push myself to sit on the edge before forcing myself to stand.

Everything hurts as if I spent a night in a boxing ring, not in a bed with Luca.

Heat floods my core at just the thought of his name. It aches like the rest of me. The thought of him taking me again makes my thighs squeeze together, but hell knows I need the release. I didn't think he'd follow through. I didn't think he'd be able to because I was right on the edge time and time again, but somehow, he knew just how to play my body and every single time I was about to fall, he stopped me.

Holding onto the vanity unit, I lower myself to the toilet to pee, the tenderness of my delicate parts not surprising me as I wipe. What I'm not expecting, however, is what stares back at me when I stand in front of the mirror to wash my hands.

I look like I've been mauled by a rabid dog.

You were.

Lifting my hand, I run my fingertips over the red hickeys that run down my neck and litter across my chest and down onto my breasts.

I don't even remember him giving me most of these, but they look like I should have because they're so bright, the skin tender.

Stepping back to get a look at my lower half, I find more of the same, only when I get to my thighs, the hickeys are joined by actual bite marks, some of which have broken the skin.

"Jesus, Luc," I mutter, running a fingertip over one of the worst ones, a memory flickering in my mind of him between my thighs and giving it to me.

There is one thing I remember though.

He never kissed me. Not once.

Pain pierces my heart at the knowledge.

I wasn't good enough for him to kiss.

A sob erupts from my throat.

He really does hate me.

We used to spend hours making out as kids, it was my most favorite thing to do, well... until we started getting a little more adventurous. I didn't realize it last night, my brain was too distracted by him and the alcohol but I needed it. I needed his lips on mine.

Wiping the tears that have spilled from my eyes with the back of my hand, I reach for the toothpaste that's sitting beside the sink and squirt some on my finger to freshen up my mouth.

My temples pound steadily as I stand there. The shower calls to me, desperation to wash away some of last night down the drain is almost too much to deny, but having none of my own stuff stops me. Then another thought hits me.

I have no clothes.

I walked in here wearing a bedsheet and a pair of panties, both of which he ripped from my body.

Grabbing a towel, figuring it's my only option to hide the car crash that my body is right now.

The bedroom door is already open, so I slip through it in search of Luca. I know he's still here. I know he wouldn't have just left me here for someone else to find.

And I soon find that I'm right when I round the corner and find him passed out on the sofa wearing only a pair of black boxer briefs.

His tattooed arm is thrown over his head, making the muscles in his torso tighten in the most delicious way.

His eyes are closed, his dark lashes resting down on his cheeks. His full lips are parted as his shallow breaths pass. Lowering myself to the coffee table before him, I sit and just take him in.

Noting all the differences from the boy I used to know.

His body was always a work of art. His dad ensured he was always in peak condition so Luca could follow his footsteps into the NFL. Even back then, his six-pack and V were well defined. But now, they're downright deadly.

His hair falls down onto his brow, making my fingers twitch to move it back, to feel its softness against my skin. But I can't. If I touch him. If I wake him, I'm never going to get out of here.

Ripping my eyes from his face, I track the lines of his abs before dropping lower.

I gasp when I discover that his cock is straining against the fabric of his underwear and my mouth waters.

The image of dropping to my knees, of pulling it out and sucking him while he's asleep fills my mind and my core throbs once more with its missing release.

How long would it take to wake him like that?

I'd like to think that one day I might get a chance to find out because I already know that today isn't the day. He already thinks I'm a slut. Him waking to find me doing that is only going to confirm his suspicions.

But the truth is, there isn't anyone else in the world I want to be a slut for. No one has ever turned me on or affected me in the way Luca does. Even when he's being wicked, even last night when the most sensible thing to do would have been to run, I couldn't.

I gave my heart, body, and soul over to him years ago, and he never gave it back. I fear that he never will and that I'll always be bound to him in some way.

Knowing that I need to do something before he begins to stir, I push from the coffee table and swipe up his discarded jersey then head back to the bedroom.

Dropping the towel to the end of the bed, I slip his shirt over my head. His powerful scent gives me pause for a second. My need to be wrapped in his arms instead of his number consumes me.

I'd give anything for him to tell me that he believes me and to hold me. Anything but risk the person I need to protect from all of this. Anything but that.

Finding his pants abandoned on the floor, I don't think twice about shoving my hand into his pockets to locate both the key to my freedom and my cell that he stole last night.

With both in hand, I tiptoe back through the main living area, grab my purse from the floor and head for the door.

I push the key into the lock and twist but the damn thing doesn't budge.

"What the—"

"Nice try, baby."

His deep voice, rough from sleep, vibrates

through me, and damn it if my nipples don't immediately harden.

"Did you really think I'd allow you to slip away from me so easily?"

I blow out a long breath.

Yeah. Yeah, I did.

"I need to go home, Luca. I've got work and—"

"You've called in sick."

His words finally make me move and I spin toward him, forcing my eyes to remain on his face as he sits on the arm of the couch, almost his entire body naked for me to feast on once more.

"I'm s-sorry, I've what?"

"You're sick. They won't be expecting you tonight."

Anger surges through me turning my blood to lava.

"You can't do that," I screech. "I need that job. I need that money."

He pushes from the couch and begins stalking toward me.

"Why, P? Why are you so desperate for the money?"

My heart kicks up a notch as he stares at me through his lashes, demanding to know all my secrets.

"I... I..." I hesitate, my gut telling me to be at least partially honest while my head screams at me to lie because he doesn't deserve the truth, especially not after last night. "I need it to pay medical bills," I blurt, my gut winning out.

His brows pull together. "Medical bills?" he asks, his eyes dropping down my body as if he's now only just going to notice I've got a limb missing or something. "But... you're perfect."

His admission floors me but I force myself to move past it because from the widening of his eyes two seconds after the words pass his lips, I'm assuming he didn't mean to say them out loud.

"T-they're not mine," I explain but immediately regret it. I'm opening myself up to too many questions.

"Okay, so whose are they?"

"Family."

His eyes narrow. "Your mom or sister then," he surmises.

This time it's my turn to narrow my eyes in suspicion.

"Or my gran?" The reality is, she died only a year after we all moved to South Carolina to live with her, but the only way for Luca to really know that would be for him to have been keeping tabs on me and I really don't think he was.

"Oh, yeah. So..."

"I'm not discussing this with you, Luc. I just need to leave."

His smile isn't at all welcome. There's no friendly happiness in it, it's purely wicked and full of dark intentions.

"You can't keep me locked up in here like some kind of sex slave, Luc. That's insane."

"You're right. I'd much rather have you chained up in my own bedroom, but we're here now so this will have to do."

My jaw drops. He's joking, right?

But his face is deadly serious.

Jesus, have I totally underestimated this new Luca?

"So you've spent the past few weeks stalking me at work and now you're what, holding me against my will?"

He closes the last bit of space between us, the heat of his body burning through his jersey and making my skin prickle with awareness.

Reaching out, he cups my chin in his hand and tilts my head up to look at him.

He lowers his head as if he's about to kiss me and I have to force my eyes to stay open, because I know he's not going to. And I'm right, because he stops only a centimeter from my lips.

My chest heaves with his nearness, my head spinning as his scent fills my nose and reminds me of the things he did to me last night. I swear to God, each hickey and mark on my body burns hot just thinking about his lips and teeth on me.

"Against your will?" he asks, his lips ghosting over my cheek until they brush against my ear. "I think you're exactly where you want to be, baby."

A violent shudder rips through me and he chuckles, clearly noticing my reaction to him.

"Yeah, exactly as I thought."

Selfishly, if I'm being honest with myself being with Luca again, even if he is this cold, brutal version of himself is where I want to be. But I can't be selfish, I have people relying on me. People who need me present and not locked up by some crazy boy I used to know.

"I need to go home, Luc," I plead.

"To him?" he spits, pulling back from me.

I bite down on the inside of my lips to stop me from spilling the truth.

"I need to go home."

"You're going nowhere yet. I'm not done with you."

I want to scream at him to look at the state of me, to tell him how much he's hurting me both physically and mentally but I don't. I fear he wouldn't hear a word of it even if I did.

"I'm hungry," I whisper.

"Go and shower. You smell like sex. I'll find you some food and coffee."

My argument is on the tip of my tongue but it's pointless. Nothing I say is going to convince him otherwise. I just need to bide my time until he screws up and I can make my escape.

He'll always find you now you're here, a little voice says in my head. He's clearly on a mission with an outcome in mind, he's not going to stop until he's achieved whatever it is.

14

———

LUCA

W alking into the bathroom, I swipe my jersey from where she's abandoned it on the floor before stepping into the shower.

Steam fills the stall, stopping me from getting a good view of her, it's probably a good thing. If I get a shot of her naked ass body right now then there's a chance I won't leave for food, or ever, to be fair.

Reaching down, I palm my hard cock through my pants.

Last night should have been enough. I fucked her seven ways from Sunday, took out all my hate, anger, and disappointment on her but one look at her trying to escape and wearing my fucking number and all I could think about was getting inside her again.

Peyton was always smart. That's how I knew she'd go straight for the key the second I passed out. And that couldn't happen. I wasn't allowing her to get away until I'd had my fill of her, even if that meant calling in a favor at The Locker Room to get her out of her shift tonight. Like fuck is she turning up with my marks all over her body.

If I had my way, she'd never go back there again, but short of getting her fired, I'm not sure how I'm going to achieve that.

The water cuts off as I'm still standing there reminiscing on our previous night and how many times I brought her right to the edge, only to leave her hanging. Every time I felt bad. That's not the way a woman deserves to be treated in the bedroom—or anywhere to be fair—but then I would remember what she said to me that night and I'd leave her high and dry, listening to her complain as her body lost its grip on the impending release.

Sliding the door open, she steps out in a cloud of steam and the second it clears, our eyes lock and my heart jumps into my throat.

Fuck, I want to kiss her. I really want to fucking kiss her. It took every ounce of restraint I possess not to claim her lips last night, to make her mine, to remind myself of just how good it used to be spending hours just making out with her.

"Luc," she gasps, her arms lifting in an attempt to hide from me.

"A little late for that, don't you think?"

She looks down at herself, color hitting her cheeks.

"I'm going out. Be good." Spinning on my heels, I

walk away from her, only to hear wet footsteps racing after me.

"You're..."

"Going out," I repeat.

"You can't just leave me here. I have no clothes, no anything."

"You don't need anything. I'll bring back food."

"Great," she mutters, and I know that if I were to turn around fast enough, I'd catch her rolling her eyes at me.

Pushing the correct key into the lock, I twist it and feel it release for me.

"Luc, you're not actually serious right now."

"Deadly. See you later."

Slamming the door behind me, I quickly lock it back up, not that I really think she'd come running out here naked to try to stop me, and suck in a deep breath.

Looking back over my shoulder, I catch her lifting her hands to her hair, and tip her head to the sky as if she's praying for strength. I stand there for a few long seconds just watching her, allowing myself to get completely fucking addicted to her once again.

"Hey, man. Good night?" Owen asks me from the deck where he's leaning against the railing smoking.

I glance back at the pool house to make sure he can't see anything before walking up to him.

"Yeah, man. Pretty fucking fantastic."

"Yeah, the hickey on your neck confirms it," he says, nodding to where the mark is.

I remember the exact moment last night when she sank her teeth into me after I pulled out of her, not allowing her to come.

"Listen, I'm not done with the pool house. Keep your boys out for now, yeah?"

"Bro, tell me you've got some girl tied to the bed or some kinky shit."

"Can't tell you my secrets, man. Just keep every motherfucker out, yeah?"

"You got it, man. Whatever you need."

"I'll be back later. Just gonna give her a few hours to really miss me."

Owen holds his fist out for me to bump and I happily return the gesture.

"Later," I say with a quick salute before taking off around the side of the house to find where I abandoned my car when I arrived last night.

I don't need to walk into our house to know it's full.

"Fucking hell," I mutter, scrubbing my hand down my face as I realize that I totally spaced on today's bowl game.

That's what she does to me. She makes me forget everything, and hell if I don't like being in that little bubble with her.

Pushing through the front door, an eruption of shouts and cries come from the den where they're watching the game.

Silently, I slip into the kitchen and kickstart the coffee maker, desperate for the caffeine hit I promised Peyton and never delivered on.

As the scent of the beans fill the room, I briefly wonder if I've done the wrong thing. Guilt about abandoning her there begins to tug at my chest, but then I think back to the way she tried to rip my family apart, the pain I remember all too well as she lied to me, and I tell myself that leaving her there alone is nowhere near what she deserves.

It's not like I've abandoned her somewhere horrible. She's in a fully stocked fucking pool house to the biggest and wealthiest frat on campus. There really are worse places to be stuck.

"Oh, look what the cat dragged in," Leon drawls, placing his beer on the counter and leaning his ass back against it.

His arms cross over his chest as he stares at me.

"What?" I bark.

"You get lucky last night?"

"What's it to you?"

He scoffs.

"Jealous? How long's it been since you saw some action who wasn't a distressed friend needing a distraction?"

"Fuck you, man. That's got nothing to do with you."

"Yet who I was with last night has something to do with you?"

162

"When you're acting like a fucking asshole, yeah. It is."

"Well, in case you hadn't realized, you're not our father and you can't tell me what the fuck to do."

My blood heats at even the mention of his name and the things he tells me to do. Although, I'm not sure even he would be able to keep me from Peyton right now.

"Speaking of, you need to call him back."

"I'm good, thanks." I already know how that conversation is going to go.

"We need to talk about plan B, Son, seeing as you royally fucked plan A with the shittiest season I've ever seen. Do you even remember how to throw a football?"

I shake his words from my head. I don't care about him, I don't care about his opinions. I got what I wanted, I'm not heading for the draft. Although I never wanted a failed season to be the reason for it.

I know it's pointless but there's a part of me deep down that just wants him to tell me that it's okay, that we all have off days, off seasons, and that there's always next year. I just want him to be proud of me. To be the dad I always hoped was hiding deep down, but at every turn, he just disappoints me. I want it to stop, I need it to stop.

I just... I think of Peyton, of the things she confessed to me.

They can't be true. They just can't. I refused to believe it back then and I still refuse to now, because if it's true then... I lift my hand to my hair, tugging on the lengths until it hurts.

It can't be true.

"Luc," he sighs, rubbing the back of his neck. "I'm worried about you."

"Yeah, well you don't need to be. Everything is great," I lie. The reality is that my life right now feels like sand slipping through my fingers. I've barely got a grasp on reality. Things are getting clouded by darkness faster than I can control.

The only thing that makes sense is her.

Tormenting her, teasing her, punishing her.

She lied and she left me to drown in the knowledge, that's something I don't think I'll ever be able to forgive her for.

He stares at me, not believing a single word. I don't blame him, I wouldn't believe it either.

"Whatever. I'm going to shower."

I'm almost at the door with my mug in hand when he speaks again.

"Who was she, Luca?"

"No one. She's no one."

I storm from the room and up the stairs before he can respond. The pain of that confession tightens my chest until it feels like my lungs are about to explode.

She might be no one now, but she was someone. Someone who meant more to me than anyone else in the world. There were times I'd even have put her above Leon.

I shake my head at my thoughts. I was so fucking stupid.

"Never put a girl above your boys, Son. All they do is try to poison your mind and distract you from what's really important." Dad's words rattle through my brain. I can't count the number of times I've heard them, or similar, over the years.

Slamming my door so hard the floor beneath me shakes, I put my mug down and begin stripping out of my clothes, desperate to wash her off me. Needing just a few moments where I'm not surrounded by her and the confusion she's brought down on my already fucked up life.

15

PEYTON

The asshole never returns and when I walk out of the bathroom, once again only wrapped in a towel, I find what I already knew. He's gone.

"You're a fucking asshole, Luca Dunn," I scream into the silence.

I don't need to try it, but I do anyway, wrapping my hand around the door handle and twisting it as hard as I can in the hope it releases. It doesn't.

"Fuck," I hiss, tucking the towel around me tighter.

Hooking my fingers into the blind, I lift one of the slats and look out.

The sun is already high in the sky, telling me that it's later than I thought but there's no one to be seen.

I could shout, scream and slam my fists against the glass, but it would be pointless. No one is coming to my rescue.

My stomach growls, reminding me that Luca promised me food. The naïve little girl inside me wants to believe that he left to get some, but I know I'm only bullshitting myself. He hasn't left to do anything nice for me. He's left to torture me.

Something in a heap on the floor next to the table that he fucked me over last night catches my eye. Walking over, I pull the hoodie up and hold it to my nose.

It's Luca's.

Dropping the damp towel, I pull it over my head and wrap my arms around myself.

With each second that passes, my headache only gets worse with my lack of liquid and with no other choice, I make my way to the kitchenette to see if there's anything in here.

To my shock, the cupboards are full and in seconds I have the coffee maker working its magic and a huge bag of chips in hand. Not exactly the healthiest option but it's exactly what I need right now.

I curl myself into the corner of the couch and rip into the bag, stuffing a handful of salty chips into my mouth.

Luca was right, I did think—hope—that he would take one look at me and forget everything that happened and that we could just move past it.

Last night, I hoped that maybe he could fuck the hate out of his system. Take all of it out on me and exorcise everything, and this morning we'd be able to start over.

I don't think that's what happened, damn it.

I came to terms with our romantic relationship being over long ago, but our friendship is harder to let go of. All of my childhood memories include him. All the best parts of my life include him.

I was stupid. Deluded to even consider the fact he would want to have me back in his life, but with everything else falling apart around me, it was easy to cling on to.

Well, no more. When—if—he comes back, I'm getting the hell out of here and turning my back on him.

He doesn't deserve me to try, and he certainly doesn't deserve the truth. And as sad as that makes me, I'm also relieved I didn't spill all my secrets the second I first saw him because he's not worthy of knowing the truth.

Once the bag is empty and my coffee is gone, I push up from the couch and set about trying to figure out an escape plan. I figure there must be an unlocked window or a spare key or something somewhere.

But as the sun begins to descend for the night, I realize that I'm fucked. I have no clothes, no cell, and no fucking hope.

I've got to sit here until the jerk returns or hope someone else turns up for something.

Pulling one of the books I found from the shelf, I

settle myself back onto the couch to wait it out. It's not my usual genre of choice, I'm a romance girl really, but a good thriller could be exactly what I need right now, it might give me all the answers I need for my escape, as well as a few ideas for how I can cause Luca a long painful death for doing this to me.

I quickly get lost in the pages but as engrossed as I am, it's not enough to keep my eyes open when my exhaustion from my lack of sleep the night before begins to consume me.

I awake with a start sometime later, blinking against the darkness and lifting the heavy weight of the book I fell asleep reading from my chest.

"Holy shit," I screech when I look forward and find Luca watching me. My hand covers my racing heart as I try to calm down. "Did you just touch me?" I ask, noticing that my skin is burning.

He shrugs, the indifference on his face causing anger to explode inside me.

"What the hell is wrong with you, Luca?" I scream, jumping up from the couch and storming away from him. "You're acting like a fucking psycho locking me in here like some prisoner." I throw my arms up in frustration and begin pacing, needing to do something to expel the energy that's racing through me.

"You didn't seem to mind so much last night," he mutters, his eyes following my every move.

"Last night I was drunk, Luc. I was fucking

wasted and—" I slam my lips shut, not wanting to allow the next words out of my mouth free.

"And..." he prompts, lifting a brow.

"And..." I sigh. "And I thought it might help. I thought you might fuck me and—"

He throws his head back and laughs. It's not the response I was expecting. "Fucking hell, P. You really must have a high opinion of your pussy if you think a night of pounding it was going to make me forget everything." My lips part in shock. "I mean, it was good. One of the best I've had in a while." His words are like a knife through my chest, and I fight to keep my expression blank so he can't see how much he's hurting me. "But it wasn't that fucking good."

"Fuck you, Luca. Fuck you." I take off running toward the bedroom, needing some distance from him after ripping my chest wide open with his cruel words. But he's faster than me and his giant hand wraps around my upper arm, stopping my retreat.

"No, Luc. No," I scream, my arms hitting, slapping, and punching any part of him I can reach.

He allows me to hit him for a few minutes before he takes my wrists in his hands and slams me back against the wall, pinning them above my head.

"Are you about done?" he snarls.

"No. Nowhere fucking near," I hiss.

Both our chests heave as we stand only inches apart, staring at each other.

I search his eyes in the hope I'll find just a flicker

of the boy I used to love hiding within the angry depths, but there's no sign of him.

"What happened to you, Luc?" I whisper, regretting the words the second they pass my lips.

His jaw tics and a muscle in his temple pulsates.

"You," he spits. "You happened to me."

"I didn't fucking do anything, Luc. I just told you the truth."

He shakes his head. "No. No, he wouldn't do that."

"Okay," I sigh, totally defeated by all of this. "If that's what you want to believe, then fine. But let me go, let me get on with my life. Spend the rest of your life living in denial and wondering if you should have believed me all along."

His eyes narrow at me. "It's not that easy, baby."

That final word rolls through me, causing goose bumps to erupt across my skin but I refuse to let it sink any deeper.

"You've done your worst, you dished out your punishment. We're done."

Taking both of my wrists in one of his hands, he grips my chin with the other and holds my stare.

"We'll never be done, Peyton. You never should have come back here."

"You think I put myself in this position by choice?" I laugh but it's bitter, full of pain and sadness. "My mom died, Luc," I confess, my knees threatening to give out as the words pass my lips. "I sat by her side and held her hand as she died."

His eyes soften slightly, but it's too late. I don't want his pity now that he knows that tiny bit about my life.

"I watched her take her last breath and leave me behind. I had no choice but to walk away from my life and start over. I'm drowning in medical debt." Most of them aren't from Mom, but he doesn't need to know that right now. "All I'm doing is trying to survive. Trying to put one foot in front of the other and ensure I have a future. What I don't need is this bullshit from you. I'm sorry you don't believe me, that's your choice. But I get to choose too, and I'm fucking done, Luc." Tears burn my eyes but I refuse to let them fall, to allow him to see just how fragile I am right now. Putting on a brave front has been my coping mechanism for weeks. I don't want to finally shatter in front of him. "What we had is dead, I see that now. All I ever did was be the best friend I could to you, but clearly, that didn't mean as much to you as it did to me."

"Pey—"

"No," I seethe, tugging my arms so harshly that he has no choice but to release me if he doesn't want to hurt me again. "It's too late. It's over."

Slipping from between him and the wall, I continue toward the bedroom.

"Peyton?" His voice is deep, rough, and full of a pain that I understand all too well but it's not enough to make me turn around and after a second's pause, I step into the room and close the door behind me.

The second the lock clicks into place, a sob erupts from my throat and the tears I was trying so desperately hard to keep from falling from my eyes finally drop.

My back slides down the door until my ass hits the floor and I fold my arms around my legs and let myself break for the first time since I sat beside my mom's freshly dug grave and said goodbye to her for the final time.

I don't hear his footsteps over my cries, but I startle when he knocks.

"Peyton?"

I sniff and try to force down the lump that's clogging my throat.

"Go away, Luc. I don't need you anymore. I learned to live without you."

Not wanting to be so close to him, not trusting myself not to turn around, open the door and fall into his arms like I once would have, I stumble toward the bed and crawl under the covers.

I have no idea how long I lay there in a ball sobbing, or at what point Luca moved from the door, if he even did. But eventually, I drift off into a fitful sleep full of nightmares that wake me up more than once covered in sweat and desperate to outrun my demons.

I wake feeling as exhausted as I did the day before but instead of my entire body aching, it's just my eyes that sting after the inordinate amount of time I spent crying for everything I've lost.

My body begs me to turn over, pull the sheets over my head and force myself to get some more sleep, but I know I can't.

I've got a life and a certain unreasonable man to deal with.

I might have let him take over my life the past thirty-six hours, but I'm done. The girl who rolled over and let him take what he needed, let him lock me up in here like a prisoner, is long gone.

Today I'm taking back control because fuck him.

Fuck him.

I open my eyes ready to take on the world, or at least Luca Dunn, and scream when I once again find him staring down at me.

"What the fuck is it with you watching me sleep?" I bark, my fingers curling around the sheets.

He's sitting with his back resting against the headboard, his arms casually resting at his sides as if he was patiently waiting for me to wake because he actually wanted to see me or some bullshit. But none of that is what really captures my attention. That would be the fact he's sitting there with messed up bed hair and clearly only wearing a pair of boxers.

"Tell me you did not sleep in here with me," I demand.

His eyes bounce between mine for a few seconds.

"Okay, I didn't sleep here."

"Don't try to be cute, Luc. It doesn't suit you. Not anymore."

He shrugs and it infuriates me.

Throwing the sheets off me, I rush to pull his hoodie down my body that I'm still wearing to cover up the fact I'm bare beneath.

"I'm going home, and you're going to let me walk out of that door."

His eyes eat me up, lingering on my bare legs for a few seconds too long before he shifts on the bed.

"Is that right?"

"Yeah. I meant what I said last night, Luc. We're done. You took your hate out on me, you used me, punished me. We ar—" His hand quite obviously slips under the sheets as I rant at him. "What the hell are you doing?"

"Your fire makes me hard. Always did."

My chin drops as my eyes take in the movement beneath the sheets.

"Unbelievable. Fucking unbelievable."

"If you wanna help me out, I might even make it worth your while this time."

His nice act doesn't fool me for a second.

"I'd rather fuck a corpse."

His eyes widen at my response.

"Your loss. You could really do with letting go."

"No, asshole. What I need is to go home and get

back to my life instead of being locked in here with you," I spit. "I stupidly thought that there could still be something here for us, but you've shattered all that hope. You're nowhere near the same person I once knew. This new version of you, well... he's a cunt, Luc. I fucking hate him."

I swing the bathroom door closed so hard I'm surprised it doesn't fall off its hinges.

I scream in frustration, not caring that he can hear me.

I pee, brush my teeth with my finger, and rip the door open once more. I hesitantly look at the bed, dreading what I might find, but to my relief, it's empty. Instead, I find him pulling his jeans up his legs.

"I want my cell and I want you to unlock the door."

He looks up as if he wasn't aware that I was here, although I know he does.

"Fine."

Opening the closet behind him, I watch as he taps in a code to a safe and produces my cell.

"Key?" I demand, holding my other hand out.

His eyes hold mine for a beat, conflict battling within them, although I have no idea what he's confused over. He hates me as much as I do him now. Why could he possibly want to keep me here when he's made it perfectly clear how he feels.

After long, agonizing seconds where I feel like he might just be about to say something that's going to shatter all of my resolve, he places the key in my hand.

"Thank you. Me and you. Whatever this has been. It ends the second I walk out that door. You get on with your life and I'll do the same with mine." I'm aware that this means having to cut ties with Ella and Letty, seeing as they seem to be his friends, but I've only known them a few days, it shouldn't be that hard.

I spin on my heels and storm away from him, swiping my purse from the counter as I pass the kitchenette on my way to the door.

I'm halfway across the living area when a loud knock on the front door sounds before it rattles violently.

"Luca, I know you're in there. Come and open the fucking door," an angry yet familiar voice calls.

"Fuck," Luca barks behind me, clearly knowing exactly who it is.

"Too late to be ashamed, Luc. You should have listened to your conscience a good few hours ago."

Not even bothering to look back at him, I march toward the door. This time when I twist the key it actually works before Leon barges inside not a beat later.

He scans the room quickly before his eyes land on mine.

They go wide almost instantly before he does a quick lap of my body.

"Peyton?" he breathes in total disbelief.

"Hey, how's it going? You need to put that asshole on a leash."

"Shit," he breathes, lifting his hand to the back of his neck. "Fuck. How are you?" he asks, showing more concern in that one question than Luca has since the moment he found me in The Locker Room before the holidays.

"I... I'm leaving." I sidestep him and am almost free when his hand shoots out, wrapping around my wrist and stopping me.

"Has he hurt you?" Leon whispers, his brows drawing together in concern.

"It's probably best you stay out of it. It's over now, anyway. Bye, Lee."

"Peyton, wait." Luca's voice sends a violent shudder racing through me.

I hate myself for it, but for some reason, my body still reacts to him quicker than my head.

"I'm sorry about your mom."

I wait for another second as a ball of emotion climbs up my throat once more before I take off.

It might be early January but it's already late enough in the day that I don't immediately freeze, only being in Luca's hoodie.

I'm at my car and safely inside in only minutes. I hit the lock button and open my purse, needing to know what Aunt Fee's response was to me not coming back this weekend before I rock up at home looking like this.

Aunt Fee: You deserve to let your hair down, Peyton. Enjoy yourself. Don't worry about a thing.

"Easier said than done, Aunt Fee," I mutter to myself as I quickly scan the messages I've received from Letty after not responding to her first one that Luca read out to me.

I don't reply. I can't. What the hell would I even say? I can hardly tell her the truth. *Or maybe you should*, a little voice shouts. Maybe she'll be able to fill in some of the gaps I have with how my sweet caring Luca turned into the monster who's locked me up this weekend.

"**Y**ou need to start fucking talking," Leon demands after watching Peyton flee from the pool house like her ass was on fire.

"Fuck you, Lee. I don't owe you an explanation for anything."

"You did just see Peyton, your old girlfriend, run from this place wearing nothing but your hoodie and looking like hell, right? Or am I fucking imagining things?"

"It's none of your business," I say, finally pulling my shirt on.

"Like hell, it's not. What the fuck is going on?"

"Nothing." Stuffing my wallet and cell into my pocket, I barge past him.

"You're not just running away from this, Luca."

"Fucking watch me."

I'm out of the pool house before he catches up to me, his palms landing on my shoulder blades and forcing me forward. I stumble but manage to catch myself before I face-plant on the ground.

"What the hell?" I boom, somehow managing to dodge his first punch. Sadly, I'm not as on the ball for the second one and his fist connects with my jaw.

"Fucking asshole." Surging forward, I plant my first hit into his stomach, causing him to double over so I can get the upper hand.

The two of us go at it like we haven't in a very long time and it's not until one of the Kappas notice and emerge from the house that we're finally dragged apart.

"You're fucking everything up, Luc," Leon hisses at me through his heaving breaths.

"It's my fucking life, I can do what I want." I go for him again but the hands wrapped around my upper arms stop me.

"You act like none of the rest of us have problems. Pull your head out of your fucking ass, bro. You're not a kid anymore."

"Fuck you." I shrug off the hands that are holding me and storm away, lifting my hand to my split lip and wiping the blood away as I do.

My knuckles scream in pain, my face aches, but it's what's inside my chest that hurts the most.

Leon's right. I am fucking everything up.

"FUCK," I bellow, slamming my hands on the wheel of my car the second I drop into the seat. "FUCK, FUCK, FUCK." I repeat it over and over, but it never makes me feel any better.

My one reprieve from all of this shit just walked away from me. What the fuck do I do now?

I allow the vibration of my car to flow through me as I suck in a few deep breaths in the hope it might help clear my head. But it does nothing.

My knuckles split open as I wrap my fingers tightly around the wheel and pull away from the frat house right as Leon stalks around the side of the building.

I don't want to go home, but I don't know where else to go.

Letty is my first thought, but like fuck will she want me showing up at her apartment like this and there's a fucking solid chance that Kane will be there, and I really don't fucking need that.

With no other choice, I take a right and speed out of Maddison County. I need to put this place behind me for a few hours.

The drive helps clear my head somewhat but the persistent pounding of my eye socket and cheek keeps me from forgetting what happened before I left Maddison. The sight of the blood coating my knuckles does a pretty good job too.

I don't park on the driveway of the main house. I don't want to be seen by more people than I have to be in this state. Instead, I kill the engine, step out onto the sidewalk and slip around the main house to the pool house in the backyard.

The second the windows come into view, I

breathe a sigh of relief when I see the little family inside all sitting on the floor playing together.

It's not until I'm at the door and pushing the handle down that I'm spotted.

"Holy crap, Luc. What happened?" Chelsea cries, jumping up from her spot on the floor, dragging me inside. "Sit," she demands, pointing to the couch before running out of the room, I'm assuming to get the first aid kit.

"What did you do?" Shane asks, moving the toys toward Nadine to keep her occupied while he grills me.

Ripping my eyes from his concerned ones, I stare down at my beautiful niece. She's seven months old now and literally the most perfect thing on the planet.

I was as shocked as the next person when we discovered that my little brother had knocked Chelsea up, but I can't deny that what they made together wasn't worth all the stress and drama.

"How's my girl doing?"

"Nice try."

Nadine stuffs a toy into her mouth and starts chomping down.

"She's teething. Had us both up all night. So..."

"Lee and I got into it."

"Again? You two haven't fought this much since we were kids," he says, knowing that only weeks ago we were at it over Letty, although our fight that night wasn't this brutal.

"What can I say, he's an asshole."

"I mean, yeah. That goes without saying but..."

"I don't want to talk about it. We both said some shit, it got messy."

"So it's over a girl again then I assume?" Chelsea asks, rejoining us and taking the seat beside me on the couch as she opens up the first aid box and pulls out what she's going to need.

"What makes you say that?"

"Just tell me it's not Letty again," she begs. "She's with Kane now. She's happy. She doesn't need you—"

"It didn't have anything to do with, Letty, *Mom.*"

She rolls her eyes at me.

"I'm worried about you, okay? Shoot me."

"We're all worried about you. Mom especially. Can you at least return her call at some point, it might stop her nagging at me so much?"

"Everything's fine. It's—"

"Don't bullshit us, Luc. We know everything isn't fucking fine or you wouldn't be here right now looking like that. Is it Dad?"

"When isn't it about Dad?" I mutter as Chelsea presses a cool wipe to my lip, making me hiss.

"Sorry."

Shane knows better than anyone what Dad can be like. When he found out about Nadine, and Shane's plans to only attend MKU part-time this year and not to even attempt to be a part of the team, he went nuclear. But before long, as it always happens when it's to do with Leon or Shane, Dad lets it go and just turns his frustration toward me as if I'm the one who's personally fucked him over.

I get it... I think. I'm the quarterback, I'm the one to possibly follow in his footsteps, to hit heights that he never managed to in his career. But fuck... I'm not actually him and his overbearing, controlling, asshat-ness is just too much to fucking bear.

I stare at my little brother, wondering how much to divulge. He'll remember Peyton. She basically lived at our house growing up, but he never really had anything to do with her, and he certainly doesn't know anything about the circumstances under which she left.

In the end, I decide to go with honesty, or at least a little of it. I know that Leon will only rat me out later if I don't confess now.

"Peyton is back."

"Pey... oooh."

"She's at MKU. I just... I wasn't expecting to ever see her again, you know?"

Chelsea continues working to clean up my face and I have to force myself to sit still while she does it and not knock her hands away from me.

Maybe coming here was a bad idea.

But then Nadine makes this cute little gargle noise and I look down into her giant green eyes and I realize that it's exactly where I need to be.

"Let me finish cleaning you up then you can hold her," Chelsea says softly, clearly sensing that what I really need right now is cute baby cuddles with the most precious little girl in the world.

Silence falls between us as Chelsea starts to work on my knuckles and Shane pulls Nadine onto his lap. They both might be young, but fuck if they aren't the most incredible parents. That little girl has no idea how lucky she is.

"Here," he says, handing his daughter over.

"Hey, baby girl. How's it going?" I ask, looking down into her sparkling eyes. Her lips curl up in happiness and she giggles, wiggling about in my arms. "Yeah, I'm happy to see you too."

Chelsea and Shane both get up and leave me with my girl for a few minutes before bringing over cans of soda.

"So I'm assuming it wasn't a happy reunion?" Shane says, unfortunately wanting to know more.

"No. When she left, we weren't on good terms."

"I remember. But that was what... five years ago? You were just kids then. Don't you think that it's time to let go of whatever it is?"

As he says the words, I find myself fifteen years old sitting in Peyton's backyard discussing plans for our summer when she turned to me and dropped the bomb that would not only change our plans for the summer, but for the rest of our lives.

Everything we thought we were going to have together was gone the moment I looked her in the eyes and called her a liar.

Pain slices through my chest as I think of the look

on her face when I adamantly told her that I didn't believe her, that she was lying to me. I had no idea why she would do that, why she'd want to hurt me, but that was the only thing that made sense because the possibility of her being right... I couldn't—I can't—deal with it.

"I don't know if I can."

"What did she do?" Chelsea asks, turning to look at me.

My lips part but I soon find that I have no words. "It... it doesn't matter."

"Exactly," Shane announces. "So just let it go. You two were so good together. I really thought this was going to end up being your life." He points to Chelsea and then Nadine.

"I don't think so, I know how to fucking wrap it," I joke, raising a brow at him. Although, it's a big fat lie because I fucked Peyton bareback without a second thought Friday night.

Out of nowhere, the image of her belly swollen with my baby pops into my head and my breathing falters. I bet she would look so fucking beautiful.

My grip on Nadine tightens as I try to get control of myself.

"Whatever. I just don't think it's worth getting yourself fucked up over. You've got enough to worry about with the new season and classes and—"

"You sound like Dad."

"Nah, man. I don't mean it like that. No girl is worth going at it over with Lee."

"Nice," Chelsea mutters.

"Baby, you know exactly what I mean. Bros over hoes." He winks and she groans.

"It doesn't matter. I don't think she's going to be making an effort to talk to me again anytime soon anyway."

"What did you do?" Chelsea asks.

"The specifics don't matter," I say, already ashamed of my actions this weekend. "We hashed out a few things and it got a bit... brutal. Lee was pissed. It was all just a bit intense."

"Right, well... Chelsea's parents are out and we were about to order dinner. You staying?"

My stomach growls right on cue. It was late by the time Peyton woke earlier, with the fight and the drive here, it's the first time I'm realizing that I haven't actually had anything yet.

"Yeah, if it's okay with you two."

"Of course. But don't get any ideas about crashing here. Firstly, unless you're going to be on Nadine nighttime duty, trust us when we say you wouldn't want to be here, and secondly, don't even think about running away from your issues. That's not how we deal with shit."

"Yes, *Mom*," I deadpan, rolling my eyes at my little, yet seemingly wiser, brother. I guess it's true what they say, becoming a father makes you grow up fast.

17

PEYTON

My heart is in my throat as I walk into work later that night. I might have been able to cover up the marks on my body enough to hide them from Aunt Fee and Elijah after managing to slip into my room before either of them caught me doing the walk of shame, but the men here —my boss—are a different story.

None of them are going to be impressed by the marks he left behind on my skin.

I'm meant to be the innocent one. That's what earns me decent money without having to accept any of the offers I get to go and make use of one of the back rooms.

I shed my hoodie and stuff it and my purse into my locker and give myself another once over in the mirror. I went all out with the outfit in the hope it would distract from the amount of concealer I've had to slather on my body.

My pleated skirt just barely covers my ass. If I bend over even slightly, then the entire bar is going to know what color my panties are, and my white shirt is unbuttoned but tied in a knot between my breasts, showing off as much skin as possible.

I hate it. I hate that men's eyes are going to be drilling into me all night. That just as Luca said, they're going to be imagining all kinds of things every time they look at me.

But that's okay, they're not going to be close enough to touch.

I tell myself this over and over as I make my way out to the bar, my skin prickling with awareness as I move.

"Whoa, girl. Someone is feeling better," Bry says, his eyes eating up my mostly exposed body.

"And on a mission," Helena mutters, also noticing me.

I just about manage to hold in my groan of frustration that she's on shift tonight.

Bry slides my water over before nodding over to my shoulder in the direction of a booth I avoided at all costs as I walked through.

"You'll be glad you put the extra effort in when you see who's waiting for you."

"What are they doing here?" I hiss. Tonight was already going to be bad, I really don't need Slick and Eyebrows here making it worse.

"Yeah, they're here but they're not the only ones."

I stare at Bry, thankful that Helena has walked off

to thrust her fake tits at some guy, so she doesn't witness the panic that races through me.

Please God, tell me he's not here.

Sucking in a deep breath, I risk a glance over my shoulder at the farthest booth back. And sure as shit, there he is.

It might be dark, I might not even be able to see his face in the shadows, but I know it's him and I know he's watching me.

"Jesus fucking Christ, he needs to leave."

"Yeah, he does. If Julian finds out that you've got a boyfriend in here. A boyfriend who is Luca Dunn, I might add, then he's going to lose his shit."

"Luca isn't my boyfriend."

Bry raises a brow at me making me wonder just how much he knows. I sure as hell have never said anything to him about Luc. He figured there was once something between us from our first meeting here. The tension was palpable, Luca's blatant threat too loud for him to miss. But I shot him down every time he brought it up after and refused to talk about him ever since.

Apparently, none of that matters though, because, from the way he's looking at me, I'd say he's well aware of the situation. Well, as much as anyone on the outside can be. I'm in the middle of it and I have no freaking clue what's going on.

"Riiight," he sings with a smirk.

"If you've got something to say, just say it."

"He waits for you every night, Pey. He cares about you."

How the hell does he know that?

"Trust me, he really doesn't. He's just trying to make my life hard."

"By trying to protect you from those assholes?" Bry sends a look to my most dreaded table.

"He is the asshole."

"What happened between you?"

"Nothing," I snap. "Pass me my pad, I've got work to do."

"Want me to tell Helena to leave his table to you?"

"No," I shout a little too loudly. There's no way in hell I'm walking up to his table and taking his freaking order. "She can have him. I hope he enjoys her."

I'm gone the second I have my pad in hand and make my way over to my fan club.

"Well damn, looks like tonight was the right night, boys," Slick says, practically drooling as I come to a stop at their table.

"How are you all this evening, gentlemen?" I purr, putting on my best act that makes my stomach turn in disgust.

If Luca thinks I'm a slut who sells herself for money, then why would I want to disappoint him?

I spend way longer than I usually would at their table, stroking their egos and allowing them to get their fill of me.

They all stick to the rules of no touching the girls,

but I see their fingers curling into fists with their need to reach out.

My skin itches at the thought of feeling their touch, but right now I want to hurt Luca more than anything else, so I push through it, finally excusing myself to collect their order.

"You're playing with fire, girl," Bry warns, slipping back behind the bar as I approach.

"Whatever. I'm just here to do my job and make some cash. The rest is white noise."

"You might not be saying that when Dunn takes out some of Julian's best customers because of the way they look at you."

"He wouldn't."

Bry levels me with a stare, knowing as well as I do that Luca wouldn't bat an eyelid at doing just that.

"Fucking hell."

"You need to deal with your shit. If Julian gets one whiff of this, then you'll be sacked faster than Helena gets the guy's dicks hard."

"So he'll give me ten minutes to explain."

Bry throws his head back and laughs. "Yeah, something like that."

I know he would. I might have only been here a few weeks, but already I've witnessed how cutthroat our boss is when it comes to things—boyfriends—upsetting business.

"He has no right to be here. He has nothing to do with me. You kick him out."

He holds his hands up in defeat. "I am not getting involved in this."

"Well, I'm not going over there."

He holds my stare.

"Okay, fine," I whine, throwing my hands up in frustration. "After I've delivered these."

I walk over to another couple of tables to collect up empties and take some orders before taking the tray Bry has put together for my dreaded table and taking it over, putting extra sass into my hips just to be a bitch. I know Luca is watching my every move. His eyes burn into my back.

"Here you go, gents. Would you like anything else?"

"You know we would, sweetheart," Eyebrows says, a disgusting smile curling at his thin lips.

"I'm sorry, that's not on the menu."

"It's a damn shame," Slick adds. "I think we could all really have some fun."

All?

I have no idea how I don't lose the contents of my stomach right there and then.

Fucking pigs.

"Right, well. Enjoy your evening." I give them my most seductive smile and thankfully slip away, although I know I'm still very much the object of their attention.

I shudder when I get to the bar but I don't get any rest because Bry slides a glass over to me.

"For your solo admirer."

I swallow down my nerves at the thought of having to look him in the eyes once more and lift the tray.

I try to convince myself that walking up to Luca right now is less terrifying than that group of sleazeball men, but it's really not. They can objectify me all they like. I don't care what they think of me. But Luca. Shit. Back in the day, his opinions used to mean everything to me. I used to care what he thought.

I shove that teenage girl deep down in the box she belongs in and hold my head up high as I step into the darkness that surrounds his booth.

There's a very good reason why this booth is situated in Helena's section. None of us can see what happens back here and we're not brave enough to come and see.

Stepping up to him, I slam the glass down on the table, making the contents splash over my hands.

"You need to lea—" My word falters when I get a look at his face.

Concern washes through me, but I bite it back.

He deserves whatever Leon threw at him for the game he played this weekend.

But as I stare at him, I don't feel vindicated in any way. I just feel... sad.

I might have been dragged away from Luca years ago. I thought I'd dealt with the loss, but deep down there was always a hope that one day we might just be able to reconnect. That he would still be the boy I remember all too well.

But he's not. That boy is dead, and the intense wave of grief that rushes through me almost takes me to the floor.

"You need to be careful with those assholes," he says as if I'm some naïve little girl who's not aware of the situation I've put myself in doing this job.

I know the risks. But right now, the benefits of the paycheck outweigh them.

Maybe if he cared a little less about himself, he'd have a better understanding of why I'm doing it.

"I know what I'm doing."

He sits forward, his elbows resting on the tables, his fingers laced together and covering what looks like incredibly sore, busted-up knuckles. His eyes hold mine. There's a softness in them that I really don't want to see. I don't want or need him to be nice to me right now. I need him to be the evil, vindictive asshole he's been since he first found me in here a few weeks ago.

"You don't have—"

"No, Luc. You don't get to show up here and do this," I explode, guessing where his question was going. "You don't get to care all of a sudden because you don't like the way they look at me, not after how you've treated me. After this weekend, I'd actually prefer to be serving their drinks and allowing them to look down my top rather than I would you," I spit. It's a barefaced lie but he doesn't know that.

"You don't mean that."

"Don't I? Do you know what else?" I ask, ready to really rub salt into his wounds. His lips twitch as if he wants to say something but I beat him to it. "I bet they'd more than willingly get me off too."

His palms slam down on the table, the glass I placed down only minutes ago rattling with the force.

"You need to leave."

"If one of them—"

"Save it, Luca. It's too late to pretend to care. You've already proved how little you feel for me now."

"They don't get to fucking touch you, P. *No one* gets to touch you."

"Oh get over yourself, you conceited jerk. Leave or I'll get security to throw your ass through the door."

"It's cute that you think they could."

My teeth grind as I barely contain my anger at his arrogance.

Reaching out, he takes his glass and tips back the amber liquid, swallowing it down in one.

The thought of him driving drunk fills me with dread but I refuse to be the kind of person who points it out now. He doesn't need me to look out for him.

"As you wish, but I'll be waiting."

"Bite me," I bark at his retreating back, but instantly regret it when I see his shoulders lift with amusement.

"Oh, baby. I fully intend to."

"I hate you," I seethe.

"No, you don't. You just hate that you're still desperate for the orgasm I kept from you."

"That's long forgotten," I spit, although from the way my pussy clenches at just his words alone, I know my statement is far from the truth. "You weren't that good, most of it was faked."

He chuckles, finally shooting me a look over his shoulder. The heat in his eyes threatens to burn me from the inside out.

With a single nod, he walks away from me and finally out the front door.

I breathe a sigh of relief until I look down at his table to collect his glass and I find a hundred-dollar bill and a note.

There's always another way.

Crumpling up the note, I throw it in the trash can behind the bar before pocketing his money. It's less than I would have earned in tips last night so it's the least he could do.

"Loverboy gone?" Bry asks, amusement filling his tone.

"He's no—" I blow out a frustrated sigh. "Whatever. I don't care what you or anyone thinks."

With every hour that passes, the place only gets busier and by the time I get off, the balls of my feet are pounding from the height of my shoes and I can barely keep my eyes open. The short nap I had at Aunt Fee's before my shift was nowhere near long enough to deal with the number of assholes I've been subjected to tonight.

Tugging my hoodie up my arms and zipping it right up to the neck, I throw my purse over my shoulder and head out.

The music still plays out from the bar and the sound of the men's chatter filters down to me. The bar stays open later on the weekends, but thankfully, I don't have to work until closing. Which is a bonus because it means I don't need to deal with the drunken idiots who don't want to go home to their wives.

I know he's there the second I step out the back door and into the parking lot. A shiver runs down my spine as my feet sink into the gravel beneath them.

Other than that one night, he stays in his car and watches me from the darkness. But everything changed this weekend.

The second I round the corner, I see him and my heart leaps into my throat.

Instead of sitting in the shadows, his headlights are on, illuminating his dark figure sitting back on the hood of his car.

His eyes follow me as I make my way to my own car to get the hell out of here.

I expect him to push off, to walk over and do something.

But he never does. He just watches me.

My hand trembles as I pull the door open and after holding his stare for a beat, I throw my purse inside and drop down into the seat.

I force myself not to look in the rearview mirror to see what he's doing and just focus on starting the engine and leaving.

I manage it until the very last minute, once I've got the car in drive and ready to go.

"Fuck," I hiss when I find he's moved and is now behind the wheel and ready to follow me out.

Putting my foot down, I speed out of the lot, desperate to be in the safety of Aunt Fee's house.

Thoughts about going elsewhere so he doesn't follow me back there flicker through my mind, but it's pointless. He already knows where I live. He saw me that night with Elijah. All I'd be doing is putting off finally getting into bed by messing with him.

With a loud sigh, I head for home, trying to ignore the fact his headlights follow me all the way there.

18

LUCA

My knuckles split once more as my grip on the pen in my hand tightens.

I should be focusing on whatever my professor is saying, but I can't get the image of her in that little skirt last night out of my head.

I might have only been in The Locker Room with her for a short period of time, but it was enough to have the image of her bending over to pass her asshole customers their drinks burned into my brain.

The thought of all the other douchebags in that place seeing the same thing made me fucking murderous.

She's mine.

Mine.

I fucking hate that she's working there. And the fact she clearly has no idea who actually owns the place because something tells me that she'd have run a mile if she knew the truth.

Our dad is nothing if not protective of his public image, so it's hardly surprising that he's not openly announced his involvement in a seedy chain of sports bars that litter the country. I always wondered why he didn't make them just sports bars but then I guess he'd lose the majority of his customers who only come for the waitresses and the extras they offer behind closed doors.

Confusion swirls around me as I once again think about what Peyton told me that night five years ago. I've been so adamant since, that she was the liar, but I can't deny the facts.

I wanted to believe that she was lying because I couldn't cope with the alternative but now she's here, openly standing before me and calling me out on it, I can't help but wonder if I did have it wrong all these years.

But if I was wrong and she was telling the truth, then it would mean that my dad... the man I've looked up to all my life is a...

I scrub my hand down my face, pushing the thought aside.

No.

No. It has to be lies.

Our father is a lot of things. But he's not that.

He wouldn't. He just wouldn't have done what Peyton claimed he did.

My head is still a fucking mess after hours in the gym after my classes. By the time I walk up to the front door of our house—a house paid for by our father—not only does my body ache from the beating I took from Leon, but my muscles pull from my workout.

My eyes are heavy, my body sluggish as I make my way to the kitchen for some food before I crawl into bed and crash.

I barely slept last night. All I could think about was her and *them.* I couldn't help wondering at what point she'll realize that she can make even more money to pay off the debts she has by allowing them to take what they want.

I want to believe that Peyton really isn't like that. But then I'm sure every woman thinks that until the offer of the money they so desperately need is right there for the taking.

"Bro." Leon nods when he walks into the kitchen behind me as if he was waiting for me to get home. If he wants to give me a lecture then he really can stick it up his ass because I am not interested in anything he has to say.

He doesn't know anything about the situation between me and Peyton, and as far as I'm concerned, the less he—and anyone else knows—the better. I won't have any member of my family's name dragged through the mud because of some teenager's accusations. Our father might be a cunt, but he's our father, and I'd protect him to the end, if it came to it.

Thankfully, the first words he says aren't to attempt to rip me a new one again.

"You've got a visitor."

My initial thought is that it's Peyton but then I get over myself and realize that she's never going to willingly come anywhere near me after the weekend.

"Fuck, really?" I ask, reading the truth in his eyes.

"Apparently he's had enough of your bullshit too."

"Fucking hell."

Reaching in the refrigerator, I pull out an energy drink, although I wish it was vodka for the conversation that I'm sure is about to commence.

With a weary sigh, I pass Leon and head out into the hall to find my guest.

"Take whatever he says with a grain of salt," Leon says behind me.

"Easy for you to say, he's not constantly riding your ass about being better."

"You're right because being forgotten is so much better."

My lips part to respond but I quickly find I don't have a comeback for that.

Leon tries not to let it bother him, but I know it does. I never asked to be Dad's favorite. I don't want to be the focus of all his attention but sadly, it's the way it is, and both of us just have to find a way to deal with it because it's not going to be changing anytime soon.

Walking into the den, I find him sitting on the winged back chair that's usually reserved for me and

Leon, with one leg bent over the other and his arms crossed over his chest.

As approachable as ever.

I fight not to roll my eyes at him but it physically pains me.

"Son," he says, nodding but not bothering to get up or anything as I fall down onto the couch opposite him.

"What do you want?" I grunt, knowing that he's not here to catch up. He's here to grill me about the season and my failed chance to enter the draft this year.

I was expecting it to happen in person over the holidays, but it turned out that he fucked off to Hawaii with some hot piece of ass that's meant to be a replacement for our mother. She's a fucking bargain bucket Barbie doll, if you ask me. I hope he knows what he lost when he started fucking around on the woman who stuck by all his bullshit. Mom's just another reason why I want to believe he's innocent in Peyton's accusation, because she's already dealt with enough of Dad's infidelity. Finding out that it is true would kill her.

"That's not the way to greet your old man after all this time," he mutters.

I sit forward, waiting for him to get to the point. He doesn't do social visits, so he can cut the fucking act right now.

I hold his eyes, begging him just to get it over with so he can leave, and I can drown every word that he's about to say to me in whatever bottle of poison I find in the kitchen first.

"You fucked up, Son."

My body tenses at his words.

There's no, tough season, or you can't win them all, with Brett Dunn. You either win or you fail, there is no middle ground. It's one of many things I will do differently if I'm ever lucky enough to have kids of my own.

It's bullshit. Totally fucking bullshit.

All my life he's been on my ass, telling me that I'm not good enough. That I'll never be him, I'll never be as good as him or as big of a success as him. What he fails to see or understand is that he's right, I'm not fucking him and neither do I want to be because he's a cunt.

Sure, Peyton might have a similar opinion of me right now, but that's not who I am, not really. I don't usually go out of my way to make anyone's life harder than necessary. And if I end up having a football team's worth of boys in years to come then I already know that I will not give a shit if not a single one of them wants to play. They can be who, and do what, they want.

"It wasn't a great season. There were things in my—"

"Don't make excuses, Luca. You didn't work hard enough. You didn't lead your team properly."

"Things didn't go as planned," I mutter. It doesn't

matter what I say right now, he won't hear any of it, even if I accept the blame.

"Seeing as you screwed up our plan to enter the draft as a first pick—" He means his plan because mine has always been to get my degree before entering, but he doesn't give a shit about what I want.

"We need to discuss the next steps."

My fists curl, my short nails digging into my palms as my heart pounds dangerously fast in my chest.

"What I think we should do is—"

"No," I blurt, ensuring his eyebrows shoot up to his hairline.

"N-no?"

"Yeah, no. I'm fed up with having my life dictated by you." I push to stand, unable to confess this and not at least attempt to expel the adrenaline coursing around my body.

"But you want the NFL, you want the life I had," he says, looking genuinely confused that there's even a chance that I don't want that.

"That's what *you* want, Dad. You're trying to relive your lost career through me and I'm exhausted. Honestly, I don't even know if I want to play again after last season." It's not a lie. It's a thought that's almost been on repeat since walking off that field for the final time last season.

Giving up everything has been a pretty consistent thought, to be honest.

It's not just football. It's Leon, Letty, Kane. Everything.

The only thing that makes it seem achievable is her. And that's so many shades of fucked up, I don't even know where to start with it.

"You what?" he roars, suddenly jumping from the couch and coming to stand in front of me, forcing me to stop pacing. "You don't get to quit this, Luca. Dunns don't quit."

"You might not, but I'm balancing on the edge of doing just that right now."

"No, I haven't worked this hard for you to just throw it all away," he booms, the muscle I'm more than used to pulsating in his temple with his anger.

"Yeah, that's just it though. It's not about you. This is about me, about my life."

"No, Luca. It's about the future, your career, your success."

"And what if I don't want to succeed, huh? What if I don't want any of this?" I throw my hands up in frustration. "What if I never wanted any of this?"

Before he gets a chance to respond with some bullshit that I already know is going to add gasoline to my already raging inferno, I storm from the room.

Leon is standing right outside, probably enjoying himself listening to the kind of bullshit Dad never spits at him.

"Did you enjoy that?" I ask, slamming my palms down on his chest, forcing him to stumble back against the wall.

All the air rushes from his lungs as he connects with the wall but he makes no move to fight back. Whatever he sees in my eyes stops him.

"Did you really mean that? You want to give it all up?" he asks, sounding genuinely concerned, unlike our father who doesn't give two shits about how I really feel.

"I don't know. I don't fucking know anything anymore."

Ripping my eyes from his, I storm down the hallway toward the front door.

"Luca," he calls before I slam the door behind me and disappear.

"What?" I bark.

"Please, don't take this out on her."

"Get your nose out of my business, Lee. You don't know what you're talking about."

The door slams behind me, cutting off whatever response he might have had to that. I know what I said, but Lee is the only person in my life—aside from Peyton—who has ever had any clue. I fear he might have more of an idea about what I'm going through right now than he lets on.

I don't leave town this time, instead, after driving aimlessly for over an hour in an attempt to calm down, I find myself pulling into the parking lot behind The Locker Room.

Leon's parting words about not taking it out on her ring out in my head, but she's the only thing right now that makes sense. She's the only one who will calm whatever the fucked up shit is in my head.

I'm out of the car and heading toward the entrance before I've even realized I've moved. It's not until I see how quiet it is that I remember it's only Monday night.

Bry notices me first as I stride toward the bar.

"Evening. Two nights in a row. You really must be desperate."

I pin him with a hard glare. We're not friends exactly, but I've spent enough time here in the past couple of years that we're at the point of it being acceptable to give each other shit.

"You have no fucking idea, man."

Without having to ask for it, a glass of whisky is pushed toward me and I knock it back without thinking.

I glance around, not even attempting to hide the fact that I'm looking for her.

"Where is she?" I finally ask not finding her pink hair anywhere.

"She's out back. She—"

"She's fucking what?" I boom, the stool I was perched on crashes to the ground behind me. The thought of her being back there with some other guy makes me fucking crazy.

"She's on break. Jesus, Luc. You need to chill your shit. I think you know as well as I do that she's not one of your dad's usual girls. They're not usually that... innocent."

Images of her in the pool house on the weekend hit me.

Innocent my ass. That woman writhing against me wasn't a woman who doesn't know what she's doing.

My chest damn near rips open, making me bleed out over the floor as I think about her with others, about her selling herself like I accused her of.

But then Bry's words register.

"She's on break."

"B-break?"

"Yeah."

My heart continues to race as I stare at Bry's concerned eyes.

"I really think you should wai—"

I don't hang around long enough to hear his warning. My need for her is too strong.

19

PEYTON

I sit at the small table in our break room and poke a carrot stick into the hummus before me. Aunt Fee always sends me to work with a healthy snack. I appreciate it, I do. But right now, I just want a bar of chocolate or some candy.

I'm exhausted, my whole body aches with my need to curl in bed and sleep for a week. But I can't. I'm halfway through what feels like the longest shift of my life.

When I walked in and saw hardly any customers, I thought I was in for an easy night, and I wasn't wrong but easy also means boring and boring equals a long ass night.

"Ugh," I groan, dropping my head to rest on my forearm and closing my eyes for a beat.

I swear it was for just a second.

The click of the door closing on the other side of the room startles me and I sit bolt upright.

"Shit, I'm sorry. I didn't mean to fall asleep," I say in a rush, quickly tidying up what's left of my food. "I'll be right there."

A tingle runs down my spine as I stand, quickly dumping everything into my lunch bag and it gives me pause.

Realizing that no one has said anything, I stop and look over my shoulder.

My breath catches at the sight of Luca standing with his back resting against the door. But it's not his presence that startles me as much as the look in his eyes.

He looks... broken.

His green eyes are dark. The fire and hate from our previous exchanges are nowhere to be seen and the hard set of his shoulders I was becoming used to has gone. He seems totally defeated.

My fists curl as I force myself to remember everything that's happened between us this past week. I repeat over and over in my head that I don't care. That Luca the man, is evil and twisted and that I hate him. But it doesn't work because that look on his face right now, it's one hundred percent the boy I remember all too well.

"Luc, what—"

At the sound of my voice, he moves. He pushes from the door and storms over.

The chair in front of me clatters into the wall as he throws it out of his way to get to me.

"Luc?" My voice is weak and cracks with

confusion as his warm fingers grip my chin and his lips slam down on mine.

Oh God.

My heart pounds, my head spins and he kisses my lips, his tongue sneaking out to try to part them, but despite every single part of my body screaming at me to hand myself over to him, this time, my head is louder.

I can't let him do this.

I wanted him to kiss me all weekend and he refused. Why should he get to do it now just because he's decided he needs it?

The expression on his face as he stood there only seconds ago flickers through my mind as his hot hand curls around my waist, burning into my bare skin.

"Come on, Sweet P," he whispers, and I melt.

There have only been three people who've called me that in my life and it was only a few weeks ago that I thought I'd lost them all. But he's here. He's standing right here and he needs this. Hell, I fucking need this.

The next time he tries to part my lips, my restraint slips and his tongue pushes inside as he walks me backward until I collide with the wall.

I gasp, giving him the access he needs to properly deepen the kiss.

Reaching down, his hands grip my thighs and he wraps my legs around his waist, his already hard cock pressing exactly where I need him.

The promise of finding that orgasm he denied me

of, all weekend forces me to forget all of my concerns and I roll my hips against him as my hands slide over his shoulders and come to rest in his hair, dragging him closer to me.

The low moan that rumbles up his throat as my tongue slides against his sends a surge of heat between my legs.

His hands slide down my thighs until he's palming my ass, pulling me even tighter against him.

I haven't got myself off since being with him. I knew that doing so would make me go back there, make me think of his tongue, his fingers, his cock, and I couldn't bear to torture myself like that. So I've suffered through it. But right now, I need that release more than I need my next breath.

"Luc, please," I whimper when he leaves my lips and begins kissing and nipping down my jawline.

He lifts me a little higher before one of his hands leaves me and the sound of his zipper mixes with our heavy breathing.

My core clenches, liquid lust filling my veins.

Fuck, I need him. I need him so bad.

I already know that I'm going to regret this the second it's over. But even with that knowledge, I don't stop. It's too late, my body is already lost to him and what he can give me.

I tell myself that it's okay to take his, because I want it too.

I'll let him do his worst, take what I so desperately need and then I can take back control.

"So wet," he growls in my ear as he hooks his finger into my soaked panties and tugs them aside. His words only make the situation worse as my hips roll, searching out some friction. "I love how impatient you are for my cock."

"Luca," I pant when the head of his dick presses against my entrance.

My legs tighten around his waist in an attempt to force him inside but before he does that, he pulls his face from my neck and stares me deep in the eyes.

For the first time since bumping into him, I feel like I'm really looking at him. The boy I knew, the man he's really grown into. Not the one full of anger and hate that he's shown me so far.

This side of him. It's vulnerable, lost, confused.

I equally hate it as much as I love it.

"Peyton, I—"

I press my fingers against his lips, cutting off what he wants to say.

Whatever it is, I already know that I'm not in any position to hear it.

Forgetting what I thought only seconds ago, I realize that if we're going to do this right now then I need to take the upper hand. I need to be the one in control or I'm not going to survive what comes next.

This needs to be on my terms.

"Give me what I need, Luc."

"Fuck," he barks, thrusting forward and filling me to the hilt in one move.

"Oh shit," I gasp, my muscles clamping around him as my nails dig into his shoulders.

My lips part to demand he fucks me but before I manage to find the words, he starts moving.

His lips find mine once more. His kisses are brutal, almost as brutal as his thrusts hit the spot deep inside me every single time.

In only minutes, I'm racing toward the release I didn't get to ride out over the weekend.

I panic right before I crash that I read this all wrong and that he's going to drop me at any minute. But that's not what happens.

Instead, he drags his lips from mine, and whispers, "Come for me, baby," in my ear.

The low growl of his voice is the final push I need, and I fall over the edge of one very tall cliff, screaming his name as I tumble into the abyss.

"Lucaaaaa. Oh God, oh shit," I chant as wave after wave of intense pleasure races through me.

My head falls against the wall and he pulls my hips out and thrusts into me a couple more times, sending aftershocks through my body before he throws his own head back and roars his own release.

For a second, I wonder if I should have forced him to back up and ruined it for him the same way he did for me time and time again over the weekend, but I quickly decide that I'm not that petty, and also, he looks insanely fucking hot when he comes and I couldn't bring myself to miss it.

Now though... now that it's over and it's time to make a stand.

When his eyes find mine, the vulnerability from before is still there but he looks a little more settled as if he needed that as much as I did.

The expression soon changes though when I open my mouth.

"Thanks, I needed that," I say coldly, unwrapping my legs from him and giving him no choice but to lower my feet to the floor.

"Peyton?" he growls as I right my clothing and smooth my hair down.

"You can leave now. I need to get back to work." I keep my back to him as I say the words, knowing that the look on his face as he hears them will gut me.

He came here because he needed me for whatever reason and I've just told him in not so many words that I'm not interested.

I tell myself over and over again that I'm not.

"W-what?" he stutters, his shadow falling over me, but still, I refuse to look over my shoulder.

"I'm sure you can see yourself out."

I rush for the door before he does something stupid like try to touch me, or kiss me again.

"Wait... I need—"

Finally spinning around, I pin him with a determined look. "I don't care what you need, Luca. You made your feelings for me very clear on the weekend. That," I say, pointing at the wall. "You owed me that. So thanks, I appreciate the gesture. But as for anything else... we're done. Over. Finito."

His lips part to respond but I'm not having any of it.

"Goodbye, Luca. I'll get security to ensure you leave if you don't go willingly." With that said, I pull the door open and all but run down the hallway as the remnants of what happened back in that room begin to flood out of me.

I fight my sob until the ladies bathroom door slams closed behind me. I lock myself in a stall and lower to the toilet as my tears spill over.

I knew it was going to hurt. I knew it was going to be a mistake but I also knew that I needed to make a point.

I'm not some toy for him to play with when he needs to hurt someone or expel some pent-up frustration.

I drop my head into my hands and cry for everything I hoped we might be able to find again but now I know is never going to happen because as far as I'm concerned, that's it for me and Luca. I meant what I said. We're done. Over. I can just only hope that I can forget as easily.

I've still got my head buried in my hands and my panties around my ankles when the door opens a while later and a familiar voice says my name.

"Give me a minute," I say, my voice shaky and weak.

Wiping at my cheeks, I clear away my tears although I already know it'll do little to make me look any more respectful. How I'm going to walk back out there and continue with my job tonight God only knows.

Pulling my panties up, I try to put myself back together as much as I can before opening the door and facing Bry.

"You know this is the ladies, right?" I quip, but my joke falls flat on its ass because the second he looks at me, his only reaction is to frown and take a step toward me as if he's going to hug me.

"No, please," I beg, throwing back my shoulders and sucking in a deep, calming breath.

"Peyton."

"No. Don't give me that look. I'm not some charity case, Bry," I snap, unable to deal with the compassion in his eyes when I know I did this to myself.

That had to happen. We needed that one final moment. But that doesn't mean allowing it to happen and taking what he owed me didn't come at a cost.

"What happened?"

"We're done. He's left."

"You don't look like you just told him to leave." Lifting my eyes from the basin, I hold his stare in the mirror over my shoulder.

"We had some unfinished business." My voice cracks with emotion and I lift my fingers to my kiss-swollen lips, remembering just how it felt with his against them.

"You should go home. Get an early night."

"I can't, Bry. I've got a shift to finish."

"It's dead out there. I'll tell Julian you got sick and I sent you home."

"No, you don't need—"

"Peyton," he growls. "It wasn't a suggestion."

His eyes hold mine, his brows lifts and I know he's not going to allow me to walk back out there.

"Take the night off, get your head together and come back tomorrow fresh."

Tomorrow... Tuesday. God, I really don't need that again.

My heart sinks with what I already know tomorrow will hold and what will be expected of me from my favorite table.

Dread sits heavy in my stomach.

Taking this job was a mistake. This isn't who I am. But I think about the tips I've got stuffed into my bra, even from our quiet night and I remember why I'm here.

"Okay," I finally conceded, knowing that I'll need to bring my A-game tomorrow night.

"Good. You need me to walk you out?"

"N-no. I'm fine. Could you just... could you just make sure he's left. I don't think I can face him again tonight."

"Of course. I'll come and let you know if there's an issue."

"Thank you, Bry. I really appreciate it."

He smiles softly at me before spinning on his heels and marching from the room.

Bry's good people. I have no idea how he ended up here, I'm sure he's got a story of his own, but it's one he keeps close to his chest and I know better than to start prying where people don't want it.

I wash my hands and throw some cold water on my face, not giving two craps about the state of me, before holding my head high and walking out of the bathroom.

"It's all clear," Bry calls from the main bar when he sees me exit.

"Thank you," I say once again before slipping down the hallway and escaping through the back door.

The second I step into the darkness, I feel him.

"You have got to be fucking kidding me?" I mutter to myself, digging into my purse for my car keys in the hope I can be faster than him.

It's a futile thought though. I'd never outrun him and we both know it.

"Wait, please," he begs, stepping up behind me, although he doesn't get close enough to touch me which is a relief.

"I meant what I said, Luc. We're done."

"I know, I just..."

It's the defeat in his tone that forces me to turn around and I instantly regret it when I get a look into those eyes once more.

"M-my dad's in town and I—"

My entire body jolts at his confession.

"And what, Luc? You thought you'd come here and take it out on me."

"No. I needed—"

"I don't care." I throw my hands up in frustration. "I don't care about what you need, and I certainly don't care about your father. He can rot in hell for all I care." Something flashes across his face but it's too quick and I don't have the energy to dissect it right now.

"Peyton, please. I'm sorry, okay. I'm fucking sorry."

"Too late, Luc. You should have thought about that before locking me in a pool house all weekend."

"Aw, come on, it wasn't all that bad, was it?" He takes a step toward me but soon stops when my entire body tenses with anger.

"Yes, Luca. It was. There's nothing you can do or say that's going to make this any better. I was stupid to think there could be anything salvageable here."

"P," he growls, closing the space once more but I'm not having any of it.

I know I can't let him touch me. It's too dangerous.

"I'm not leaving town," I tell him before he so much as suggests it. "I need to be here. I have people relying on me."

"Peyton, I didn't even—" I hold my hand up, cutting him off.

"I'll stay out of your way," I promise before pulling my car door open and dropping into the driver's seat.

"No, please. I just want to talk. My dad, he—"

"You lost any right to 'just talk' when you called me a liar and turned your back on me, Luc. Too little too late."

Slamming the door closed, I quickly hit the lock in case he decides to try and drag me out before starting the engine and flooring the accelerator.

Stones fly up behind me as I speed past him, forcing him to jump out of my way.

My hands tremble as I fly from the lot. I don't even remember if I looked to see if the intersection was clear. It must have been because I'm not sitting in a crumpled car.

My heart is still racing and my eyes still burning with the tears I refuse to shed after leaving him like that.

It's what he deserves, I tell myself.

"Hey, sweetie. You're home early," Aunt Fee says when I walk into the kitchen to find her doing something on her laptop.

"It was dead. Bry sent me home for an early night."

She studies me for a beat. "You look like you could use it. You're doing too much," she states.

"I'm fine," I promise, pulling a bottle of water from the refrigerator and twisting the top.

"You're not and we both know it. What's really going on here, Peyton?"

I stare at Aunt Fee for long seconds, wondering just how much I want to confess. I have no idea how much she actually knows, but seeing as Mom and her shared everything, I have to assume that she knows it all.

"It's Luca," I confess, dropping into the seat opposite her.

"Oh." She lowers the lid of her computer and folds her arms on the table.

"You know you'd run into him eventually," she says softly. "How'd he take it?"

Images of our time together flicker through my mind. "Not well."

"Silly, silly boy."

"He's loyal," I mutter, thinking of his refusal to accept the truth.

"Yeah, to the wrong person."

Her eyes hold mine, giving me all the answers I need. She knows everything.

"I just wish..." I trail off, not really having the words to finish that sentence. I wish for so many things. That Libby stayed out of trouble, that Luca believed me, that Mom exposed the truth instead of running away. But mostly, I just wish I could have my best friend back. I haven't found anything even close to the connection the two of us shared, and I miss it.

A sob rips from my throat.

"Oh, sweetie."

"I miss him, Aunt Fee. I miss him, I miss her. I just..." I blow out a calming breath. "Everything is such a mess. All I want is a decent life for Kayden but—"

"You can't ruin your life trying to make that happen, P. Kayden does have a good life. Despite everything, he's happy. He likes it here and he's making incredible progress."

"I know but he could have so much more, you know."

She nods sadly. "I do. But like I told you before, that's not just down to you. I can only tell you what I think."

"And that is?" I ask, already knowing that I'm going to regret it.

She holds my eyes, her own sparkling with unshed tears. "There's too much loss in this world. You of all people know that Peyton. Life is short. Everyone deserves all the family they can get."

I nod, the lump in my throat too big to speak around.

Lifting my bottle to my lips, I force down large gulps before looking back at her.

"And if they don't accept him?"

"But what if they do?"

I slide down in the chair, allowing my head to hang back.

"I'm scared, Aunt Fee," I confess, staring at the ceiling.

"I know. I am too. But you don't need to expose him straight away. If they refuse to accept it, then nothing has changed for him."

I know she's right, but the thought of them—of him—telling me again that he doesn't believe me, that he wants nothing to do with Kayden. It shreds me.

"I want him to be worthy of knowing Kayden."

"I know you do. I only want the best for that little boy too, you know that. But maybe knowing about Kayden will allow him to prove his worth. It might be the push Luca needs to finally pull his head out of his ass with this."

Dropping my head into my hands, I consider standing in front of Luca once again and confessing everything. But just like every time I've thought about it over the years, I'm immediately fifteen again listening to him telling me that I'm a liar and that he couldn't believe we were ever friends.

"I need to go and shower," I tell Aunt Fee, standing with my bottle and heading for the door.

"Just think about it, yeah?"

Like I think about anything else. "I will," I agree before dragging my weary body up the stairs for what I already know is going to be a fitful night's sleep once again.

20

PEYTON

Much to my surprise, when I open my eyes the next morning, I actually feel like I've slept, which is a relief.

I dress and throw my hair up into a messy bun, seeing as I fell asleep with it still wet last night and head downstairs.

Aunt Fee is in the exact same place I left her last night, the only difference is that her breakfast is in front of her, not her laptop.

"Good morning," I sing, putting as much joy into my voice as possible.

"PeyPey," Kayden sings, excitedly bouncing in his seat.

"Hey, my gorgeous boy. Did you sleep well?" I ask, dropping down beside him.

"I missed you," he confesses, making my heart ache.

"Aw, I missed you too, baby boy." Leaning over I

plant a sloppy kiss on his cheek and ruffle his hair. "See, didn't miss me that much, did you?" I joke when he fights to get away.

"Breakfast?" Aunt Fee asks, pushing from the table.

"Sit down. I can sort myself out."

"Nonsense. You're going to college with a good meal in you this morning," Her eyes drop down my body. "You look like you need it."

I smile at her. I'll be the first person to admit that I haven't been eating right in a while. Well, not since Mom died and my life got flipped on its head once more.

With a stomach full of bacon, Aunt Fee and Kayden wave me off from the sidewalk as they head in the opposite direction for the store and some winter sun.

My heart is in my throat throughout the entire drive to MKU. I hated to do it yesterday, but I turned up to class at the very last minute and I left the second our professors had finished in my attempt to avoid the grilling that I know is coming from Ella and Letty.

I don't need to have read the messages that were sitting on my cell Sunday when I finally got it back to know that they are both suspicious as fuck as to what's going on.

And now I know that Letty is close to Luca, well... it makes me want to talk to her even less.

It's a shame because they seem like my kind of

people. But I refuse to be the girl who puts herself in the middle of friends and tears people apart. Luca might not agree, but ruining people's lives isn't really my MO.

I pull the same stunt this morning, waiting in my car until the last second when I make my way across campus to the Westerfield Building, knowing that I share my morning class with Letty.

Unfortunately, it seems she's caught on to my little plan because when I slip into the room barely five seconds before our professor, I find her sitting in the closest row with a spare seat next to her.

"Good morning," our professor booms through the auditorium ensuring everyone's—bar Letty's—attention turns to him. Letty keeps her eyes firmly fixed on me, her brow lifting as she briefly glances down at the space beside her.

"Nicely played," I mutter when I drop down into the empty seat.

"Can't play a player," she mutters, flipping her notebook and writing down the title our professor has just displayed on the wall.

To my surprise, she doesn't say anything for the entire class. But I'm not naïve enough to think that's not because she's not got a million and one questions. I can practically hear them all spinning around her head.

It's not until our class draws to a close and she picks up her purse to put her things away when she finally speaks.

"You should have told me that you were Luca's Peyton."

"I'm not Luca's anything," I hiss as I throw my books and pen into my purse.

But it seems that my tone doesn't put her off because the second I stand and move toward the exit, she follows.

"The second he stepped up behind you on Saturday night, all the pieces fell into place."

"I'm amazed he never mentioned my name," I mutter, following the stream of students down the hallway.

"He didn't."

"Ouch." But as much as that might hurt, it's exactly what I expected.

"But people talked about you, compared me to you. Apparently, I never quite lived up to the enigma that was Peyton Banks."

"You expect me to believe that?"

She shrugs.

"I think we need to go and get a coffee, and properly talk."

"I need to go to the library. I've got an assignment to do," I lie.

"Not happening. Ella is busy, and me and you need to sit down and hash a few things out."

I go to argue with her but the second I glance over, I watch as she lifts her cell to her ear.

"Hey," she says, a smile twitching at her lips.

"Yeah. Coffee shop. Ten minutes? Great. See you there."

"Who was that?"

"Someone else who wants to talk."

"Why do I feel like this is an ambush?"

"Probably because it is."

"Great."

"Aw, come on. It's not that bad. We're just worried about Luca and we think you probably hold all the answers."

"Prior to a few weeks ago, I'd not seen him for five years."

"That may be true, Peyton. But I'm pretty sure he's never really let you go."

She gives me a small reprieve as we walk toward the coffee shop and instead of grilling me about Luca she turns the conversation to work.

We order and find ourselves a table before the person she was speaking to on the phone appears. I know the second he walks in because the volume of chatter dips.

Glancing over my shoulder, I guess I shouldn't be surprised to find Leon stalking our way.

"Morning, ladies," he says, wrapping Letty in a bear hug when she stands to greet him. "Peyton," he nods when I don't make a move to receive the same welcome.

Leon and I were never close. Just friends because of mine and Luca's closeness. I'm sure we could be friends though, we just never really got the chance.

He twists the chair around and sits on it backward, pulling his coffee that Letty bought for him closer.

"P tell you about her weekend then?" He asks, looking between the two of us.

I shake my head.

"I was waiting for you," Letty tells him before they both turn their eyes on me.

"Jesus," I mutter.

"We just want to help," Leon says, sincerity bleeding from his tone.

I stare down at my coffee for a moment. If they expect me to spill all mine and Luca's secrets then they're going to have to think again because that's not going to happen. Leon clearly has no idea what happened between us and it's not my place to tell him when Luca obviously doesn't want him to know.

"I know, but there's no need. Luca and I, we've... put our issues to bed."

Leon scoffs. "Oh yeah because that's what was going down in a bed this weekend."

"Leon," Letty chastises.

"What? Luca locked her in the pool house at the Kappa house."

"He what?" she seethes.

"Seriously, it's over. We've said what we need to say and we're leaving it all in the past where it belongs."

"Peyton, don't lie to me," Leon growls, sounding entirely too much like his brother.

I'm sure most people can't see the similarities between them, but after being attached to Luca's hips for all those years, I see them.

"I have a feeling that things will never be over when it comes to you and Luca. You've been gone years but you were never forgotten. Letty might have done a good job of filling the void, but you're a piece of him, Pey."

I shake my head, refusing to believe it.

"That may have been true once upon a time, but it's not anymore. There is no Peyton and Luca anymore. It's over."

"What happened, Peyton? How did you go from being as close as you were to... well, nothing?"

Lifting my hand, I drag my hair back from my face.

"I just... I told him something. Something he didn't want to believe."

They both stare at me with blank expressions. "Is that really all you're going to give us?" Letty asks.

"Yep."

"He came to see you last night, didn't he?"

I nod, thinking of our brief encounter in the back room at the club.

"What happened? He never came home and no one's seen him since. He's not picking up his cell. I'm worried."

"Yeah, he did and I once again told him something he didn't want to hear."

"Fucking hell," Leon mutters, scrubbing his hand down his face. "Any idea where he might be?"

"I don't know him anymore, Lee. The Luca I used to know died a long time ago."

His lips part but he swallows the words that were on the tip of his tongue as he studies me. "Do you really believe that?"

"He's not shown me any differently."

"Luca's... Luca's not in a good place right now—"

"You don't say," I deadpan.

"He told our dad that he's thinking about quitting the team, everything, yesterday."

"He did what?" Letty gasps.

"Then he came to you—"

"And I sent him away."

Leon blows out a breath and drops his head.

"Okay so... where'd he go?"

"I already told you, I don't know—"

"What?" he asks, looking up as if I'm about to provide him with the answer.

"N-no. It's stupid."

"Peyton, I can't find him. None of the guys have heard from him. Mom was already losing her shit with him and now I've alerted her to the fact he's fucked off and—"

"You remember that place we all camped at once as kids?"

"Right at the end of the beach?"

"Yeah. That's the only place I can think he'd go. But that was years ago when—"

"I'll let you know." He's gone before I get to tell him that it's probably a long shot at best.

"Fucking hell," I breathe, dropping my head into my hands.

"Everything will be okay," Letty says softly after long painful minutes.

My eyes are full with unshed tears when I glance up at her and her expression softens even more at the sight of them.

"Why don't you hate me?" I ask, genuinely curious.

She chuckles, although it lacks any actual humor.

"Luca may never really have spoken about you, but others did. Leon did. I know how big a part of his life you were. It took me a while to realize why Luca shut down whenever he was going down memory lane, but as soon as Leon explained, it made total sense. Just talking about you hurt him. He—"

"I never meant to hurt him, Letty. What I told him. It was... it was the hardest thing I've ever done. But I knew I had to do it, I knew I had to confess the truth to him."

She nods, understanding shining in her dark eyes but unlike Leon, she doesn't even try to find out what I might have said.

"You're not a bad person, Peyton. I can see that. You were just kids. Crazy shit happens." I nod, knowing that she's right. "But we're not anymore. You're a junior in college about to embark on possibly the most important years of your life. Luca is..." She blows out a breath, glancing out of the window for a second. "He was drowning before you showed up, Peyton, and that's on me. I'm as much to blame here for his spiral. I did some stuff that... it's not important right now but you need to know that this... darkness, it's not solely your fault. Your arrival has only added weight to an already sinking ship."

"I never meant—"

"I know," she assures, taking me by surprise and reaching across the table to my hand. "I know, Peyton. You care about him, we can see that. I know that from living in your shadow."

She glances up again and I can't help but wonder if we're about to be joined by someone else.

"You were right to stand your ground. You deserve better than how he's treated you. But also, give him time. He's working through a lot of shit, and if he's seriously threatening to quit football, then I fear it could be worse than I thought. But you need to make a decision."

"Oh?"

"Be there for him, or don't. One way or the other." Her serious face morphs into something else entirely as she looks up once again as a shadow falls over me. "Hey."

She's swept out of her chair by a strong tattooed arm and is soon completely distracted from our conversation when he captures her lips.

She finally manages to push him away to let her up for air and the two of them sit opposite me.

"Peyton, Kane. Kane, Peyton," she says quickly, in case we needed the reminder.

I nod at him, forcing a small smile onto my lips.

"I was right," Letty says. "She is Luca's Peyton."

"I'm not—" I start to argue again but her eyes come to mine, cutting me off. "I was... I was Luca's Peyton."

"Trouble in paradise?" Kane asks with a smirk and a little too much enjoyment sparkling in his blue eyes.

"I don't know what paradise is," I mutter. I can't remember the last time I was genuinely happy, although I know it was before Mom dragged me out of Rosewood, and I know it was because of him.

"Listen," Kane says, pulling Letty's chair closer and throwing his arm around her shoulder. "It's no secret that Dunn isn't my favorite person," Letty scoffs, making me wonder what the story is there but I don't get to pry. "But I will give you this advice. Don't go down without a fight. Make him work for it."

Letty turns to him and barks out a laugh.

"What? Got me, didn't it?"

"Because this," she says, waving her hand toward me. "Is anything like what we went through."

He shrugs, clearly seeing things differently to his girl.

"Luca hates you, right?" he asks, turning back to me.

Pain slices through my chest at his words but I

nod, because he's right. Luca does hate me, and he wants to make sure I know it.

"But he can't stay away from you?"

"I... I don't know about that."

"He locked her in the Kappa pool house all weekend," Letty helpfully supplies which amuses him.

"Well then. Just like I said, don't go down without a fight. You never know what might come out at the end of it."

He drops a kiss to Letty's temple and my heart melts at the sight.

They make it look so easy, so real, so... perfect. I have no idea what they went through to get there, but I'm pretty sure it was all worth it.

"I gotta run. I've got a meeting in the study center then I wanna hit the gym this afternoon."

"Okay. See you at home later?"

"You got it, Princess."

He leaves her with a knee-weakening kiss before nodding at me and striding from the coffee shop, taking the adoring stares of every female around with him.

"You two are too damn cute."

She smiles goofily before muttering, "Kane is anything but cute."

"He is with you."

She shakes her head. "What are your plans for the rest of the day?"

"Other than going home to hide?"

"Peyton," she sighs.

"I was planning on the library. I've got all the work I should have done over the weekend to complete."

"Awesome. Let's go."

Just like that, I find myself walking side by side with Letty and realizing that my plan to put some distance between us all so I'm not in the middle of Luca's life and friends has already gone to shit.

I briefly wonder what Leon's going to find at the place I sent him, probably nothing but old memories and the hopes of two young, naïve kids.

I blow out a long breath that Letty doesn't miss.

"Despite Kane's opinion, Luca is one of the best people I know. We'll get him through this. All of us."

My lips part to tell her that I can't be a part of that, that I'm already in deeper than I should be and hiding too much but I don't find any words.

Instead, I nod and follow her inside the building, hoping like hell that when the truth does get revealed, it won't tip him over the edge any more than he already is.

21

LUCA

Something hitting me in the stomach drags me from my fitful sleep.

"Go away," I mutter, already knowing that the second I open my eyes or allow reality to seep in that I'm going to be hit with the hangover from hell.

"Unlikely motherfucker."

I groan at the sound of Leon's voice. He moves, his clothing rustling but still, I refuse to even crack my eyes open.

My temples begin to pound as I try to ignore the fact my mouth is like the fucking Sahara.

I knew it was a bad idea. I fucking knew, but I did it anyway. It was the only way I could see out of the hell that yesterday descended upon me.

"How did you find me?"

"How do you think?" His voice is closer, telling

me that he's getting himself comfortable for the long haul.

"Fucking Peyton," I complain, hating the way my chest aches from hearing her name pass my lips.

"Talk to me, Luc." I hate the desperation in his voice. Fucking hate it.

We've never been the kind of brothers who do the heart to heart, heavy shit but it seems that might be about to change.

Unable to see a way out of this, I roll on my back and rip my eyes open.

I regret it the second the blinding sun fills them.

"What time is it?"

"Almost midday."

"Jesus."

My stomach lurches as I attempt to sit up, last night's cocktail of alcohol threatening to make a reappearance.

"Here," Leon says, passing me over a bottle of water and a bottle of painkillers. "I had the suspicion you might need them."

"T-thanks."

Twisting the top off the bottle, I down half before throwing two of the pills into the back of my mouth and laying back down.

Silence stretches out between us for the longest time. I'm trying to come up with what to say, how to even put how I'm feeling right now into words and thankfully, he doesn't push me for it.

"I have no idea what I'm doing, Lee. All this shit is

happening around me and I have no idea how to deal. Then she showed up and fuck." I lift my hands to my face, scrubbing over my skin. "I don't know. I just lost the fucking plot."

"Yeah locking her in the pool house screams fucking psychopath, Luc."

"I just..." I sit forward once more and drop my head into my hands. "Fuck."

"You never stopped loving her, did you?"

I look over at him, shocked that he's ever said the words.

"W-we were just kids, Lee. I'm not sure—"

"Don't lie to me. I was there. I saw the two of you with my own eyes. Hell, I fucking hated the two of you for a long time because of what you found."

"You did?" I ask, concern pulling at my brows.

"Yeah. I mean, I've got you, obviously. But I've never had a friend, or anything really like you did with Peyton. I was so fucking jealous."

I stare at him, floored that he's just admitted that.
"Shit."

He shrugs. "Do you really want to let that go now that she's back?"

"We're not the same people anymore."

"No one would expect you to be. Five years have passed. A lot of shit has happened. But that's not the point really, is it? Do you still want her despite whatever bullshit went down that you both still refuse to confess to?"

"I never stopped wanting her. That's not the issue. I don't know if I can trust her."

"Have you even talked about... about whatever it was?"

"No."

"Maybe you should start there instead of just punishing her for something you might not fully understand."

I look at him, stare into his green eyes that are so familiar to the ones I look into every day in the mirror.

"When did you get to be so wise?"

He shakes his head and chuckles. "I always have been, bro. You just haven't noticed before now."

"Oh fuck off." I laugh, and despite the fact it makes my head pound with pain, I can't deny that it doesn't feel good.

"And what about the rest of it? Have you had it out with Letty yet?"

"Kind of. We spoke for a bit last week."

"A bit?"

"It was more than we have in weeks."

"It's not enough, Luc. If you wanna fix this shit, you need to sort stuff out. You need to hear Letty out, listen to what really happened with Kane. It might even help you understand how you're feeling about Peyton."

"What do you know that I don't?"

"It's not my place to discuss their relationship with you. But there are bigger things than you know about when it comes to Kane and Letty. She's happy, Luc. Really fucking happy. I know we hurt you. I know Kane hates you. But it's how it is. You need to be able to accept him in her life, and in yours."

I scoff, still not happy about that unexpected turn of events at the beginning of the season.

"Which leads me to the biggest issue here. Football."

"What about it?" I spit, although I already know where this is going and quite honestly, I don't have an answer for him.

"What you said to Dad yesterday, did you really mean it?"

"I don't know. And this isn't some overly dramatic sulk because we lost, this isn't new. I've been feeling like this for a while. I'm just tired, Lee. I'm tired of the pressure, the bullshit, the expectations."

"From who?"

"Him. I fucking hate him, Lee," I confess.

"I know and I get it." I turn to look at him, ready to rip him a new one because he doesn't know, he doesn't get even half the shit I do. "Oh no, don't even think about it," he snaps before I manage to say anything. "Don't pull the 'you don't understand it's different for you card.' I fucking know it's different because I've been forced to watch it for years, Luc. I know exactly what kind of pressure he puts on you, exactly what he expects of you because while I might not be the one going through it, I'm here on the sidelines watching and feeling your pain right alongside you."

I open my mouth to argue but I have no words.

"I get it, okay. I fucking get it. And if you sit here right now and tell me that you're done with football, that you're going to walk away from all of it, then I'll support you all the way."

"Well, shit," I breathe because I was not expecting that. I thought he was going to be angry that I'd even consider walking away from it all.

"I'm not the bad guy here, Luc. I'm on your side, always."

"Did you just happen to forget that when you fucked Letty?" I mutter.

"Fuck, man. You need to let that go."

"I know. It just hurts that you both lied to me. We don't do that, Lee. We fucking don't."

"So tell me why Peyton really left town."

I stare at him, the words right on the tip of my tongue, her accusation word for word how she told it to me. But I can't do it.

"If I do, then it leaves you wide open, bro."

All the air rushes from his lungs.

"Yeah, exactly as I thought. We all have our secrets, Lee. Until I know the truth. Until I know for sure that she did lie to me that day, I'll keep it locked down. Trust me when I say that you don't need to hear the words unless they are one hundred percent the truth because if that's the case, it's going to change things for us."

He narrows his eyes studying me as if he'll be able to read the words in my head if he searches long enough.

"That's bullshit."

"You'll thank me if it turns out to be bullshit. You don't need that poison in your head. And trust me, I ain't letting you lock her in a pool house. You've already got game with my girls."

He throws his head back and laughs. "I swear to you, Luc. I've been nowhere near Peyton and I promise I never will. Well... unless she really begs."

"She can beg all she likes," I mutter.

"Aw, bro, you wouldn't even share with your twin?"

Images of the girls we've had between us over the years flicker through my mind before they morph into Peyton.

Could I do it? Could I share her like we did with those nameless jersey chasers, with Letty?

No. I'm pretty sure I couldn't.

"Touch her whether I'm in the room or not and I will fucking kill you."

"And there's the answer to my first question."

My breath catches. "Fuck you, bro. Fuck you."

"So are you coming back or is your new life plan to be a hobo who lives at the end of the beach?"

I look around at the tree-covered hideaway that I could call my home.

"I dunno. It's pretty sweet here."

His eyes lift from me and I know the second he spots it because he sucks in a sharp breath.

"How about you come back, talk to her and you can make some new memories instead of having to relive the old ones like a loser."

"I'm not a loser," I argue.

"Sure. Whatever you say."

He climbs to his feet and stares down at me.

"So?"

"I'll follow you in a bit."

He nods, taking a step back. "You'd better."

I nod and watch as he pushes a branch aside and walks away. Just before he's out of sight, I call out.

"Yeah?" he calls back.

"Thank you."

"I gotta be useful for something, right?"

"Lee, I... I really appreciate it."

"I know, bro. Just make it right, yeah. You'll never forgive yourself if you don't at least try. Sometimes, we've just got to let go of the past."

His words are laced with pain but he's gone before I get to say anything about it. I guess whatever it is he's kept covered up all these years is going to remain in the lockbox he keeps it in.

With a sigh, I fall back onto my palms and take in the view of the glistening blue ocean in the distance.

This used to be our place. A little bit of paradise for when we needed some peace from school or our parents.

Twisting around, I look at the spot on the tree behind me that Leon was looking at.

The letters P and L are carved deep into the trunk surrounded by a heart.

Climbing to my feet, my head continues to spin as I stare at my really bad knife skills.

I remember the day we did this. I truly believed it would be us together forever against the world back then. I never could have imagined that only weeks later we would be ripped apart.

With a loud exhale, I eventually pick up the bottles littered around my feet and make the walk back to my car.

I hadn't planned on sleeping out here last night. I didn't have a plan at all other than I needed to make it all stop, and the only place I could see that happening was at the bottom of a bottle.

I stop for food on the way home, shoving a burger into my mouth as I make the drive back to Maddison in the hope it soaks up whatever alcohol might be in my system. I probably shouldn't be driving right now, but I wasn't hanging around there any longer.

The house is quiet when I get back, I guess everyone is either in class or working out. That or acting like the easy-go-lucky off-season college students they are, unlike me.

It's not until I get to the third floor where mine and Leon's room are that I hear music playing from his.

I knock and push the door open before he calls out.

"Hey," I say, finding him at his desk working. "Not in class?"

"Nah, I'd have been late. I'll grab the notes off someone."

"Sorry, I—"

"Don't. It's okay, Luc. Whatever you need, yeah?"

"Yeah. I was actually going to see if you could do something for me tonight."

"Sure. What is it?"

I close his bedroom door behind me and drop down onto his bed.

"Peyton has a job at The Locker Room. That's where—"

"What?" he barks, disbelief filling his features.

"That's where I first found her on Christmas Eve."

His eyes widen at my confession. "You've known she's been in town since Christmas Eve?" He must see the guilt on my face. He places his pen down and properly turns to look at me. "Jesus, Luc."

"I went there for a drink. It seemed like a better option than pretending to be happy with you and Mom." His lips purse like he wants to rip me a new one for that but he thankfully refrains. It doesn't matter, it's too late now. "Safe to say she wasn't expecting to see me there."

"I'm assuming she has no idea who owns it?"

"No, I don't think she does. Which is why I need

you to go there tonight. Dad's in town and I want him nowhere near her."

He narrows his eyes at me. "Why? What would Dad want with her? No offense, Luc, but he probably doesn't remember her. He barely remembers his own kids most days."

"I know... I just... please? She's not going to want me there, and I don't think it's a good idea I go but—"

"That's where you've been going every night, isn't it? Keeping an eye on her."

I don't answer him. I don't think he really needs the confirmation. Instead, I scrub my hand down my face, rubbing at my rough jaw.

"I just sit in my car and make sure she leaves okay."

"You're fucking whipped, man. You know that, right?"

"You haven't seen the way those scumbags look at her. It's... it's disgusting. How I haven't killed any of them yet, I don't know."

"She needs to leave. She doesn't belong in a place like that."

"She needs the money."

"There are other ways."

"I know. I'm just trying not to get involved."

He throws his head back and laughs. "That was a joke, right? You couldn't be more involved right now if you tried."

"Trust me, I could. I could throw her over my

shoulder and demand she never step foot in that place again."

"Why haven't you?"

"Because she's working there to pay off her mom's medical bills."

"What's wrong with her mom?"

"She died."

"Oh… shit."

"So will you… just make sure she gets out, okay?"

He nods. "But I'm not doing it every night because you're too much of a pussy to sort your own shit out."

"I know. Just tonight."

"Okay. Now fuck off and go shower. You fucking stink."

"You're an asshole, you know that, right?"

"Oh yeah, because I do fucking nothing for you."

I flip him off over my shoulder, but when I look back, he's smiling just as much as I am.

"Thank you," I say again before slipping out of his room in favor of mine so I can do as he suggested because he's not wrong about how I smell.

22

PEYTON

As it has become normal, my stomach is in knots and my hands tremble when I walk into The Locker Room on Tuesday evening.

Thankfully, when I walk out into the bar, I find my dreaded booth empty. But I'm sure it won't stay that way for long.

"Hey, how are you doing?" Bry asks, once he's finished serving and comes to my end of the bar.

"I'm good. Thank you for last night."

"No problem. It seems you've got a new babysitter tonight," he mutters, passing my bottle of water over.

"Huh?"

He nods toward the table where Luca was sitting the very first night I found him here. Looking over my shoulder, my breath catches when I find Leon sitting there smiling at me.

It really shouldn't happen but one look at him

and my heart drops. After everything, I shouldn't want Luca to be here. But I do.

"Here. He needs a refill."

Bry passes a soda over and I take it over.

"Hey," I say shyly as I walk up to his table, aware that I'm wearing way less clothing than I'd like right now. But despite all the skin I'm showing, his eyes don't once drop from mine.

"Hey. Thank you," he says politely, accepting the drink I pass over. "I assume Luca sent you."

"Yeah, what gave me away?"

I laugh, but it lacks any humor.

"You don't belong here, Peyton. This." He finally looks down at me, his eyes widening. "This isn't you."

"I'm not the girl I used to be, Lee. And sometimes, we've just got to do things to survive. This is one of them."

"I'm sorry about your mom."

"T-thanks," I force out. My emotions are running high just from the sympathetic look in his eyes. "How much did he tell you?"

Leon shakes his head. "Not much more than that, other than he's been an asshole."

"Putting it mildly," I mutter, making him laugh.

"I know it's not an excuse, he's totally in the wrong here no matter what happened between you, but he's in a really bad place and you just happen to turn up at the wrong time."

"He hates me, Lee. Anytime would have been the wrong time."

"Yeah, maybe. But you're wrong. He doesn't hate you, Peyton. Far from it."

I scoff, looking over my shoulder when a commotion starts at the door. The second I find them, my eyes lock with Slick and my stomach drops. Oh good, now my night can really get started.

"You don't need to be here to babysit me, Lee. I'm a big girl and I can look after myself."

"Uh... funny, because I said the exact same thing to Luca but I think I'll stay for a bit, actually." He doesn't once glance at me as he says this, instead, his eyes are locked on the men behind me. God only knows what they're doing, I dread to think but it's clearly enough to warrant Leon feeling like he needs to stay.

"Okay, do whatever. But you can't do his dirty work forever."

Spinning on my heels, I take a step away from him.

"How much do you owe, Peyton?"

All the air rushes out of my lungs at his question. It's something I try not to think about because the reality is too depressing.

"A lot."

I take off, not wanting to hear whatever he wanted to say after. I'm too scared he'll do something stupid like offer to pay it. It's no secret that the Dunns have more money than sense, but I'm not a charity case and even if Luca and I were the best of friends again right now, I'd still refuse to take anything from him.

This is my problem to deal with, no one else's.

Leon doesn't move from his table all night and I feel his eyes on me every place I go. But it's not like having customers watching, stripping me bare and hoping I might drop something and bend over for them. Having him watching me makes me feel safe. I have a feeling that if any of the men were to step out of line that he'd get to me way before security. It's like having a brother watching me, protecting me. And annoyingly, I kinda like it.

When I emerge at the end of my shift with my purse thrown over my shoulder and thankfully a hoodie covering up as much of my exposed body as possible, he pushes his half-empty drink aside and stands to walk me out.

He doesn't speak until we're at my car and when he does, it brings tears to my eyes. I tell myself that it's just my exhaustion after a stressful shift, but really, it's the sincerity I see shining in his green depths, one I wish I could see in another pair.

"You're too good for this place, Peyton. You can't stay here. The way they look at you. The way they talk to you." His lips curl in disgust and his fists clench at his sides.

"I hate it," I confess. "But other than taking up a spot on a street corner, it's the best shot I've got at getting the kind of money I need."

I know the words are coming but they still hit like a baseball bat across the chest.

"Let us help."

"No."

I cross my hands over my chest, standing my ground.

"You could—"

"No, Leon." His face drops and I realize I might have been a little harsh. "I really appreciate all this. The offer. But it's not necessary. This is my life now, and I need to deal with my own shit. Luca made his decision five years ago. Just because I was his friend—his girlfriend—once, it doesn't mean you owe me."

"Peyton, that's not how it—"

"Leon, please," I beg. "I'm exhausted. I just need to go home and sleep tonight off. Tomorrow, we can all just get on with our lives. Thank you for tonight, but you really don't need to do his dirty work."

Without waiting for a response, I pull my car door open and drop inside.

I stare up into his concerned eyes once more before reaching out to close the door, cutting off any more conversation between us. But just before the door closes I swear I hear him say, "he still loves you, Peyton."

All the air comes rushing out of my lungs as I stare at the steering wheel, too afraid to look back at the expression on Leon's face. Although I'm not sure why. I'm not sure if I'm scared of what I thought I heard being confirmed or shattering hope that I might not have imagined it.

With what feels like lead in my chest, I put my car into drive and head for home.

I barely say three words to Aunt Fee who's still up waiting for me. Her brows pull together in concern as I grab a bottle of water and head straight upstairs to shower and collapse into bed.

I go to class Wednesday morning and then get straight back in my car to head home. The library would probably be a better option seeing as there is never peace and quiet in Aunt Fee's house during the day since Kayden and I moved in, and now with Elijah being there, but there was no way I was risking sitting anywhere on campus and risking having to talk to anyone.

I know that Leon, Letty, and I'm sure Ella, once she finds me, only want what's best for me. Our friendships might not have much—or any—history, but I know they're good people who only want to help.

It's why I really shouldn't be surprised when the doorbell rings at Aunt Fee's house when I'm helping her make dinner.

"I'll go," Elijah calls from the living room. Probably relieved to have a break from whatever Kayden is forcing him to endure on the TV right now. Kayden's infectious laugh keeps filling the house and melting my heart so I know at least one of them is enjoying it.

Elijah's deep booming voice fills Aunt Fee's small house as he greets whoever it is.

I don't give the visitor a second thought because there's very little chance it'll be for me. The only person who knows where I live is Luca and seeing as he sent Leon to be my bodyguard last night it seems he's not interested in seeing me himself. And that is more than fine by me because I'm not sure I've got any more fight left in me. I knew this semester would be hard, starting over in a new place, new classes, and all while trying to work to earn as much money as possible. Add Luca into all that and... I let out a long sigh.

"You okay?" Aunt Fee asks, looking over from where she's chopping vegetables.

"Yeah. It's just harder than I thought it was going to be."

She lowers the knife and turns to look at me at the same time Elijah calls my name.

He appears in the doorway a few seconds later. "It's for you. But if you don't wanna go, I'll happily keep the blonde entertained."

"Elijah," Aunt Fee snaps, sounding horrified, but there's a wide smile on her face. She knows all about what Marines get up to. Her late husband was one after all, and I heard a few stories about when she first met him from Mom.

"What?" He shrugs, pulling the refrigerator open and pulling out a beer. "So are you going or..." he says to me, pointing to the door.

"Uh... yeah." I wipe my hands on a tea towel and head toward the front door.

"Hey," both Ella and Letty say when I emerge.

"Uh... hey," I reply, looking between the two of them curiously.

"We hope you don't mind. We did a bit of detective work and found out your address."

"I-it's okay," I stutter, looking past them, half expecting Luca to jump out any minute.

"He's not here," Letty assures, clearly reading my thoughts.

"We knew it was your night off and we thought you deserved to have a bit of fun."

"Oh?" I ask, suddenly much more intrigued.

"It's not much but we thought you might like a trip around the mall and then grab some dinner."

Excitement fills me for the first time in a while as I look at the two women who've made an effort to come and make me feel better. I haven't had that... ever. They've no idea how much it means to me.

"I'd love to." I look down at myself in my ratty old jersey dress and leggings that are so old they're barely black anymore. "But I need to change."

"We can wait," Letty says.

"Okay." The words to invite them inside teeter on the tip of my tongue but then Kayden's smiling face pops into my head and I realize that I can't. "Let me just throw some decent clothes on and I'll meet you at your car. I'll be like two minutes."

They both look a little disappointed but I don't allow myself to dwell on it before swinging the door closed and running for the kitchen.

"Change of plan," I tell Aunt Fee. "I'm going out for dinner. Is that okay?" I ask in a rush, realizing that I'm totally bailing last minute.

"Of course it's okay. Go and have fun."

"Okay." I run up the stairs, rip my clothes off and replace my rags with a pair of skinny jeans, a plain white tee and my mom's old leather jacket I love that always makes me feel a little more like myself.

I swipe some mascara on my lashes and coat my lips in some gloss and figure that it'll have to do.

I say a quick goodbye to Aunt Fee and Elijah—who's escaped the cartoons—before poking my head in to see Kayden.

"Hey, bud. I'm going out for a little bit."

His face drops at my words and I immediately regret my decision. "But we're having dinner."

"I know. I... uh..." I look back when I sense someone join us.

"You've got the whole weekend with Peyton, Kay. Remember what Saturday is?" Kayden's face lights up as he remembers and I can't help but feel the same knowing I've got the entire weekend off work. It can't come soon enough.

"Okay," he says. "Have fun with your friends."

"I will, baby boy. Thank you." I hold him tight for

a few seconds and place a kiss on his head.

This balancing act between work, college, having a life and being a part of this family is something I need to get a better grip on. I'm just glad we've got Aunt Fee because if she didn't reach out to help us after Mom died, I have no idea how we'd have coped.

"Go," Aunt Fee says when I linger a little longer. "And have fun."

"Thank you," I mouth to her as I slip past.

She smiles at me, her eyes looking a little wet. She can never understand how much I appreciate everything she's done for us. I have no idea where to even start trying to tell her either.

"Hey. I'm ready," I say, dropping into the back seat of Letty's car that's idling on the road outside Aunt Fee's.

"That your aunt?" Ella asks, and when I look up, I find Aunt Fee watching us through the window.

"Yeah," I say with a smile.

"Okay, well. You ready to hit the store?" Letty asks, clearly sensing the heaviness in my response.

"Yes," Ella hisses. "Let's do it."

Walking in and out of each store while the two of them pick up different items, try some on and purchase others makes me feel more like myself than I have in a long time. Although I've never really had any girlfriends to do this with, spending an afternoon in the mall was one of mine and Mom's favorite ways to relax. Even if we never bought anything.

Ella's in the dressing room and Letty is looking at

the shoes when a dress catches my eye. It's not my usual style, and it's way dressier than anywhere I have to wear it but it just speaks to me for some reason.

It's simple, classic and something you could wear for years and years and would never look out of date. Christ, I sound like my mom.

Reaching out, I run the soft fabric through my fingers imagining how it might look on me. Twisting the tag, I gasp at the price.

"You should try it on," Letty says, over my shoulder.

"N-no, I can't afford it. And I don't need it. I can hardly wear that to class."

"No, but you never know, someone might take you out on a hot date."

I scoff. "Unlikely."

"You never know. Stranger things have happened."

"Hey, how's it—Whoa, that dress is hot. You should totally try it on," Ella joins in when she finds us standing looking at it.

Glancing up at the two of them, I find them standing with their hands on their hips and a determined look in their eyes.

"Just try it. It might look awful and you can forget all about it," Ella quips.

"El." Letty laughs. "It will not look awful. Peyton's got a banging figure."

"I know." She shrugs, reaching out and pulling the

correct size from the rack without even asking me. "Go on then." She smiles at me so sweetly and with so much determination that the only way to get out of this is to do it.

I blow out a breath once I'm alone in the dressing room. I know exactly what's about to happen, I'm going to fall in love with it even more the second it's on my body and I'm going to feel guilty for weeks for buying something so frivolous when I've got more important things to do with my money.

"So?" Ella calls through the curtain.

I stare at myself in the mirror, tears filling my eyes and a lump so huge clogging my throat that I can't respond.

"Peyton?"

When I still don't respond, the curtain moves a little and Ella pokes her head inside. She takes one look at me and throws it aside and invites herself in.

"Shit. Are you okay?"

I sniffle and nod, trying to get a grip on myself.

"Letty," Ella calls, startling me. In only a second, she also appears at the curtain.

"Okay, you're buying that," she states before coming over and taking my hand in hers.

"I'm sorry. Things just... things just hit me all of a sudden, you know. Mom and I, we used to..." I blow out a breath, unable to keep going.

They encourage me back so that I can sit down. Sharing a knowing look.

"Things have just been so insane since she had

the accident that I haven't really had any time, and then standing there..." I blow out another shaky breath.

"It's okay, sweetie," Ella breathes, her hand squeezing mine in support.

We sit in silence for long minutes as I try to gather my emotions.

"I think you're right," I finally say. "I need to buy the dress."

"You do."

"She'd have loved it." I smile despite the pain slicing through my chest as I think about her and the fun we had together. "She'd have demanded that we went out dancing to show it off."

"Then that's what we should do."

"It's my birthday on the weekend," I blurt, regretting it the instant both of their faces light up.

"Then we are definitely taking that dress out dancing this weekend. Why didn't you tell us?"

"I don't want to celebrate. It feels all kinds of wrong right now."

"Bullshit. Your mom would want you to go out and paint the town red."

"It's not just that, though. There's all this crap with Luca and—"

"Fuck him," Letty snaps, the viciousness in her voice surprising me. "You don't get to be miserable because of him. That's bullshit. Saturday night, we're partying."

"I promised Aunt Fee I'd spend the weekend at

home."

"That's fine. But as soon as the sun goes down on Saturday night. You're ours. She can even come if she likes."

"To a college party?"

Ella shrugs. "You know what crazy shit goes down. No one would probably even notice."

"As amusing as the idea is, I think she'd rather stick needles in her eyes."

"Fair enough."

"Right," Letty says, hopping up from where she was kneeling on the floor. "Get changed. Buy the dress. Then we're going for tacos and margs. My treat." She winks at me, and I can't help but smile.

I have no idea how I was lucky enough to find these two in all the bullshit that surrounds my life right now but I couldn't be more grateful.

With the bag containing the dress swinging from my fingers, Ella and Letty lead me toward a restaurant for dinner and we're seated in the middle of the vast space and handed menus. Letty orders a pitcher of margaritas before the server has a chance to escape along with a bottle of water for her seeing as she is driving.

They keep the conversation light and as far away from dead mothers and wicked ex-best friends as they can get.

Everything is great.

Fantastic.

Until he walks in.

23

LUCA

I spent what was left of Tuesday locked in my room. But as exhausted as I was, I couldn't shut it off. That only got worse once I knew that Peyton had started her shift.

Leon was there. I knew she was safe. But the thought of those men trying something and not being there to help her didn't sit right with me.

But I knew she didn't want to see me. She made that perfectly clear on Monday night when she used me for what she needed and then dropped me like a stone.

I deserved it. I know that. But fuck, it doesn't stop it from hurting.

I'm meant to be the one seeking vengeance after what she did. She shouldn't hold the power to hurt me. But she does. And she always has.

Despite Leon knocking to get my ass out of bed this morning for class, I didn't emerge from my room until long after everyone had left. I didn't want to deal with people and I really didn't want to go and sit in a class when I already know that I'm not going to hear a word of it.

What's the point? What's the point in any of it?

If I walk away from football like I've threatened to do, then I probably won't even have a place here at MKU.

It won't just be my football career that goes down the drain but my entire future.

Do I really want to start over?

A huge part of me says yes. To grab the chance of starting over without being controlled at every step by my father. To be me. Whoever Luca Dunn is without being QB1. I'm not sure he even exists.

Everything about my life for as long as I can remember has been about that, about the NFL, about success, about the win, the trophy, the high.

I glance at my shelf that holds all those trophies.

They mean nothing. Not really.

Sure, winning is great. Beating the other team is a rush. But that's not real happiness.

It's empty.

You walk away from that high of the win and what's left? The memory.

Okay, so I've got my team to celebrate with, and a desperate jersey chaser or two. But even that's getting old.

"Argh," I groan, shoving my head into my pillow so Leon doesn't hear me from the next room.

I hate all this unknown. All these questions.

I just want to be happy and to get on with my life, not have the past and the pressure dragging me down at every turn.

I startle when a knock sounds out on my door a few minutes later.

"You ready?" Leon asks, dressed, ready to head out.

"Err..."

"Colt's birthday."

"Fuuuck," I grumble, wrapping my hand around the back of my neck and pulling.

"I'm not making up a bullshit excuse about you being ill. You either pull your head out of your ass and come or you tell him yourself."

Since freshman year, we've always gone out for each other's birthdays. It's a tradition I started. One I wish right now that I really fucking hadn't.

Back then, I was gunning for the starting quarterback position and would do anything to show my leadership and to prove that I deserved it.

Now I'm considering handing it all over.

"Fuck, yeah. I'm coming. Give me ten."

I might be fucking up everything about my life right now, but I refuse to force my bullshit on the rest of the team. They might all be gutted about how our season ended but they're already getting ready to start all over again in a few months. To prove our place and make our senior year our best season yet.

I wish I shared their optimism.

I sit in the back of Leon's BMW while he, Colt, and Evan argue about some shit I have no clue about. Ignoring them, I just stare out of the window. I might have agreed to come but no one said anything about having to enjoy myself. My growling stomach, however, is totally on board with the tacos someone mentioned earlier.

I think back to last year when we rocked up to the same restaurant—the only one Colt ever chooses should he get the option—and wish things could be just like that.

A smile twitches at my lips as I remember us all flirting with our server to try to get some tequila out of her. She must have been in her thirties. She had a wedding ring on, but I don't think I've ever seen anyone blush as fiercely as she did all the while giving us just as much shit back as we gave her.

It was a great night.

We never got the alcohol we wanted. We made up for it when we got back to the house after, mind you.

This year though, more than half of us are legal which takes the fun out of it somewhat.

I follow the guys as we make our way through the mall, earning us more than a few interested glances, points and whispers.

It's not until we're being directed to our table inside the restaurant that I bother to look up, and when I do, I lock eyes with her silver ones and I swear to God the world falls out from beneath me.

I stop, causing a couple of the guys to collide with my back and ensuring everyone else turns to look at me to see what's going on.

"Oh fuck," Leon breathes.

"I'll leave," I say, taking a step back, assuming the guys have moved.

"Where the fuck are you going?" Colt asks, totally oblivious to my life imploding.

I back up once more but he's not having any of it. His hand lands on my shoulder and he shoves me toward an empty seat directly opposite her.

I keep my eyes on her but her stare is fixed to her half-empty plate in front of her while Ella and Letty lean into her.

Letty glances up, finds me staring, and shakes her head.

Great, she's even got my friends wrapped around her little finger.

Letty nods toward the hallway where the bathrooms are and I push my chair out once more to stand.

"Where are you going?" Leon hisses.

Glancing over his shoulder, he follows my stare.

"Don't cause any fucking trouble."

"Me?" I ask innocently.

He rolls his eyes at me and I step around him.

"What the hell are you guys doing here?" Letty snaps the second I'm in front of her.

Lifting my hand, I push my hair back before wrapping it around the nape of my neck.

"It's Colt's birthday. This place is his favorite. I had no fucking clue you'd be here with her."

"She's got a name," Letty hisses.

"Fucking hell." I glance up at the ceiling, hoping I can find some strength.

"Firstly, you need to stay the hell away from her." I wipe any kind of expression off my face as I stare at her.

"I'm not a fucking moron, Letty." Her brow lifts in question. "You have no idea what went down between us. But it's nice to see you're already choosing sides."

"I'm not choosing anything, Luc. And that's rich seeing as you were the one who turned your back on me not so long ago. I have every right to be pissed at you for that alone without even mentioning what you've done to her."

"She's got a name," I quip, earning me a growl. "What was the second thing?" I ask, remembering she made her first point.

"Does Kane know you're all on a team night out without him?"

I shrug. "I don't want to be here. You think I was party to the fucking guest list?"

"Whatever. You hurt her again, and I'm coming for you."

I can't help but laugh at her serious face.

"Luca, this isn't funny. What you're doing right now isn't all that different from how Kane's treated me in the past, and you remember how you reacted to that? Well, you hurting her does the same to me. Prove to me that she's done something wrong. Prove to me that I shouldn't believe she's anything but innocent in whatever this thing is between the two of you and I'll walk away. But until you can do that, me, Ella, hell anyone who wants to be, are going to be her friend and support her. You might think you've got it hard right now, try being in her fucking shoes."

Her lips part like she wants to add to her ass ripping but she changes her mind, instead just shakes her head once before walking away from me and returning to her seat.

Whatever she says to Peyton causes a reaction because she looks up directly at me. My entire body jolts at the sadness in her eyes as if I've just taken a fucking bullet.

After long, agonizing seconds, she drops her gaze once more and continues poking around at the food on her plate with her fork.

Not wanting to cause drama by walking out, I return to my seat.

Until I've made a solid decision about my future, I need the guys to think everything is relatively okay.

"All good?"

"Letty's on team Peyton," I whisper to Leon.

"Fucking hell, bro. There are no teams here. We're all here for both of you and just want you to sort this shit out."

I nod at him, not believing a word of it.

I know how they really feel, I can see it in their

eyes. Despite not knowing anything about what happened, they all believe her. They just think I'm an asshole with a grudge that I can't get past.

Maybe I have. I don't fucking know anything right now. Maybe I have been wrong all this time and the vengeance I've so desperately craved for five years was built on nothing but my own distrust and misplaced loyalty.

"Fuck," I bark, turning all eyes on me.

Not wanting to go into it, I grab a menu and stare down at it, although all the words swirl around the page in front of me.

Sitting with her in my eye line is torture.

Half of me wants to go over and try to talk to her, but the other half still wants to hurt her for all the pain she caused me, although I can't deny that that side isn't shrinking faster than I can cope with as I watch all the people I care about quickly becoming her friend.

The thought of being wrong all this time terrifies me but Letty is right. It's time to find out for sure as to whether what she told me that day was all lies or not.

If only there was an easy way to figure it out.

Thankfully, once the girls have had their dessert, Letty pays the cheque and they get up to leave.

I've missed every single conversation that's happened around me, my entire focus on Peyton and what she might or might not be saying to Letty and Ella.

The three of them have no choice but to walk

past me to exit the restaurant. I suck in a breath as Letty and Ella surround Peyton as if they can actually protect her from me.

I don't intend to do anything but the second her scent fills my nose I can't help myself and my hand flies out, my fingers wrapping around her wrist.

"Let go," she fumes.

"Luc," Lee sighs, frustration evident in his tone.

Looking up, I find her huge silver eyes. The exact ones that have featured in my fucking dreams for the past five years.

My chin drops to say something, but I don't have any words that aren't me pleading for her to talk to me.

Now that she's in front of me, I realize that all I want is her.

My heart pounds as we stare at each other. Her eyes hard and closed off, mine begging, but I already know who's going to win because it's going to take a hell of a lot more than this after all the shit I've pulled.

"Luca," Letty snaps. "Let her go."

My fingers loosen, but before I totally let her go two words fall from my lips. "I'm sorry."

She sucks in a harsh breath but she doesn't say anything as she pulls her arm away and marches off.

"Stay away from her, Luc. I mean it," Letty warns before giving Lee a hug and following the girls out.

I'm pretty sure I've never felt smaller in my entire life.

"I'm sorry," I say, pushing my chair out. "You guys enjoy your night."

"Luca, what the hell are you doing?" Lee barks, following me out.

"Don't worry, I'm not going after her. I just... I need to be alone right now."

I don't wait for his response; I just take off running through the mall.

24

PEYTON

The Mexican restaurant was the last time I saw Luca this week. He never showed up at work Thursday night, Leon did again, and I didn't see him around campus the last two days either.

I should be glad that he's kept to his word and stayed away from me. What I really shouldn't be is concerned.

But after learning from Leon that he spent Monday night exactly where I suspected and drank himself unconscious, and then the look in his eyes as he stared up at me on Wednesday night, I can't help it.

Deep down, no matter what Luca does, what he thinks of me, I'll still always remember him as my best friend. As the sweet boy who would do anything to protect me. It's ingrained in me.

I stare at my new little black dress hanging on the

door of my closet but even the sight of that can't bring a smile to my face right now.

Today is too hard. Everything hurts too much.

Aunt Fee, Elijah, and Kayden have done everything they can so far to make it special, but Mom's absence in my life has never been stronger.

I thought I missed Libby when she went her own way, choosing a life of addiction over her family.

I drop my head into my hands. I thought I was lonely when we left Rosewood. But I had no clue.

Standing in that hospital alone, with the two people I loved most in the world in critical condition and unable to find my sister, let alone get a hold of her to tell her what was happening.

That was sheer loneliness.

It was also the only time I very nearly called Luca. The one time I almost caved to my need for the boy from my past who always picked me up when I fell, who always held me when I was hurting.

I sat for hours with his name right there, the call button taunting me.

I had no idea if it was even his number anymore. For all I knew, if it connected it could have been to some random person on the other side of the country. But in those hours where I knew nothing but sheer fear and desperation. He was the only one I wanted.

As I sit here now, thankfully being able to leave that hospital weeks later with one of those people and our guardian angel that is Aunt Fee, I wonder just what would have happened that day if I'd have gone through with it and told him the situation I was in.

Would he have come to help, or would he have called me a liar and turned his back on me once more?

The possibility of it being the latter only adds to the agony and loss that I'm feeling right now.

"PeyPey?" a little voice calls up the stairs. "Are you coming?"

"Yeah, one minute."

Sucking in a deep breath, I stand in front of the mirror and pull Mom's necklace from my jewelry box. Libby and I bought it for her one year for her birthday and she never took it off.

It's the one thing I have now that helps me to feel closer to her.

I place the white gold heart locket against my chest and run my fingers through my hair.

Schooling my features, I head out of my room hoping that my brave face will at least be enough to convince Kayden that I'm okay, and that I'm enjoying the day he planned for me with Aunt Fee this week.

"You look pretty, PeyPey," he says when I emerge in the kitchen where he's helping himself to the plates of food Aunt Fee is in the process of taking outside.

I left the plans up to Kayden and he decided that I needed a picnic for my birthday this year.

It's January, but I guess we are in Florida so it's

not so bad. Although we could be in Alaska and I'd go with it if it meant seeing him smile.

"Kayden," Aunt Fee chastises when she comes back to find him with his cheeks puffed out with food like a hamster.

"Wot?" he asks around all the food.

Rolling her eyes at him in faux exasperation, she walks over. "Shall I help you out?"

I watch them both go, scooping up the final few plates to take out.

It's totally over the top for the four of us but I appreciate the gesture.

Aunt Fee tried to convince me to invite Ella and Letty, or anyone really, but I couldn't. They're already in deeper with this thing with Luca and me than I want them to be. Them discovering the truth before he does would not go down well.

I might have told Luca the truth five years ago, but that doesn't mean I haven't kept something pretty fucking huge from him ever since. And I know that at some point I'm going to have to come clean and deal with the consequences. I just have to understand that it was about more than him or me. It's about that little boy out there. The one whose smile lights up every room he enters, and whose heart is pure gold despite the crap that's been thrown at him in his short few years.

"Oh wow, this looks amazing," I say, putting as much awe into my voice as possible when I see the banners and balloons that litter the backyard.

"Do you like it, PeyPey?" Kayden asks with hope shining bright in his eyes.

"I love it, lil' man. Thank you so much." I drop to my haunches and pull him in for a tight hug, hoping that by the time I pull away I'll have got control over the tears that are desperate to fall from my eyes.

"Right, who's hungry?" Aunt Fee asks as if she knew that I needed an out before I fell apart.

"Oh whoa," I say, genuinely shocked when I see the cake. "Did you two make this?" I ask, taking in the two-tier cake with pink icing flowers all over it.

"We did," Kayden announces proudly coming up behind me. "The icing is just like Play-Doh but tastes better."

"It's a miracle there were any flowers left to put on it," Aunt Fee jokes lightly as we all take a seat at the table.

"Happy Birthday, Peyton," Elijah says, pouring me a glass of champagne, seeing as I'm now legal.

"Thank you."

"I know it's probably not quite what you imagined for your big two-one but I hope—"

"It's perfect, Aunt Fee. Thank you so much for... for everything."

"Anytime, girl. You know that, right? Dig in. I suspect you're going to need to fill that stomach before your big night out tonight."

I laugh at her, happy to pretend it'll be the first night I go out drinking. We can all fake it every now and then.

We chat away about nonsense. Elijah talks about shipping out again in a few days and Kayden regales us with every one of his crazy stories about the things he and Aunt Fee get up to when I leave the house.

Everything is as perfect as it can be given the circumstances until the back gate slams, turning all our attention to the other end of the yard.

"Oh my gosh," Aunt Fee gasps as my eyes land on the one person I did not want to see in this house—or yard—uninvited.

"L-Luc," I stutter, standing from my chair and coming to stand in front of Kayden in a pathetic attempt to hide him.

Luca is holding a huge bunch of flowers, way bigger than I've ever received before, and a birthday card, but exactly as I suspected, I'm not the object of his attention as he closes the space between us because his eyes are locked on the little boy I'm failing to protect right now like I promised myself I would.

"Peyton?" Luca whispers as he gets closer, his brows pulling together, and without any other option, I stand aside, allowing Luca to see Kayden properly for the first time.

Both gasp in shock, able to notice the similarities in each other's faces. Similarities I've been forced to look at every single day since Kayden was born.

"P-Peyton. Is he... is he mine?"

His question slams into me out of nowhere, shock rendering me speechless for a few seconds but before

I get to respond, everything around me blurs, my head spins, and darkness consumes me as my body gives out.

Peyton and Luca's story continues in The Destruction You Desire coming 22nd July 2021
PRE-ORDER NOW

ABOUT THE AUTHOR

Tracy Lorraine is a new adult and contemporary romance author. Tracy has recently turned thirty and lives in a cute Cotswold village in England with her husband, baby girl and lovable but slightly crazy dog. Having always been a bookaholic with her head stuck in her Kindle, Tracy decided to try her hand at a story idea she dreamt up and hasn't looked back since.

Be the first to find out about new releases and offers. Sign up to my newsletter here.

If you want to know what I'm up to and see teasers and snippets of what I'm working on, then you need to be in my Facebook group. Join Tracy's Angels here.

Keep up to date with Tracy's books at
www.tracylorraine.com

Rebel Ink Series

Hate You #1

Trick You #2

Defy You #3

Play You #4

Inked (A Rebel Ink/Driven Crossover)

Rosewood High Series

Thorn #1

Paine #2

Savage #3

Fierce #4

Hunter #5

Faze (#6 Prequel)

Fury #6

Legend #7

Maddison Kings University Series

TMYM: Prequel

TRYS #1

TDYW #2

TBYS #3

TVYC #4

TDYD #5

Ruined Series

Ruined Plans #1

Ruined by Lies #2

Ruined Promises #3

Never Forget Series

Never Forget Him #1

Never Forget Us #2

Everywhere & Nowhere #3

Chasing Series

Chasing Logan

The Cocktail Girls

His Manhattan

Her Kensington

Co-written with Angel Devlin

Hot Daddy Series

Hot Daddy Sauce #1

Baby Daddy Rescue #2

The Daddy Dilemma #3

Single Daddy Seduction #4

Hot Daddy Package #5

B.A.D. Inc. Series

Torment #1

Ride #2

Bait #3

THORN

SNEAK PEEK

CHAPTER ONE
Amalie

"I think you'll really enjoy your time here," Principal Hartmann says. He tries to sound cheerful about it, but he's got sympathy oozing from his wrinkled, tired eyes.

This shouldn't have been part of my life. I should be in London starting university, yet here I am at the beginning of what is apparently my junior year at an American high school I have no idea about aside from its name and the fact my mum attended many years ago. A lump climbs up my throat as thoughts of my parents hit me without warning.

"I know things are going to be different and you might feel that you're going backward, but I can

291

assure you it's the right thing to do. It will give you the time you need to... adjust and to put some serious thought into what you want to do once you graduate."

Time to adjust. I'm not sure any amount of time will be enough to learn to live without my parents and being shipped across the Pacific to start a new life in America.

"I'm sure it'll be great." Plastering a fake smile on my face, I take the timetable from the principal's hand and stare down at it. The butterflies that were already fluttering around in my stomach erupt to the point I might just throw up over his chipped Formica desk.

Math, English lit, biology, gym, my hands tremble until I see something that instantly relaxes me, *art and film studies.* At least I got my own way with something.

"I've arranged for someone to show you around. Chelsea is the captain of the cheer squad, what she doesn't know about the school isn't worth knowing. If you need anything, Amalie, my door is always open."

Nodding at him, I rise from my chair just as a soft knock sounds out and a cheery brunette bounces into the room. My knowledge of American high schools comes courtesy of the hours of films I used to spend my evenings watching, and she fits the stereotype of captain to a tee.

"You wanted something, Mr. Hartmann?" she sings so sweetly it makes even my teeth shiver.

"Chelsea, this is Amalie. It's her first day starting junior year. I trust you'll be able to show her around. Here's a copy of her schedule."

"Consider it done, sir."

"I assured Amalie that she's in safe hands."

I want to say it's my imagination but when she turns her big chocolate eyes on me, the light in them diminishes a little.

"Lead the way." My voice is lacking any kind of enthusiasm and from the narrowing of her eyes, I don't think she misses it.

I follow her out of the room with a little less bounce in my step. Once we're in the hallway, she turns her eyes on me. She's really quite pretty with thick brown hair, large eyes, and full lips. She's shorter than me, but then at five foot eight, you'll be hard pushed to find many other teenage girls who can look me in the eye.

Tilting her head so she can look at me, I fight my smile. "Let's make this quick. It's my first day of senior year and I've got shit to be doing."

Spinning on her heels, she takes off and I rush to catch up with her. "Cafeteria, library." She points then looks down at her copy of my timetable. "Looks like your locker is down there." She waves her hand down a hallway full of students who are all staring our way, before gesturing in the general direction of my different subjects.

"Okay, that should do it. Have a great day." Her smile is faker than mine's been all morning, which really is saying something. She goes to walk away, but at the last minute turns back to me. "Oh, I forgot. That over there." I follow her finger as she points to a large group of people outside the open double doors sitting around a bunch of tables. "That's *my* group. I should probably warn you now that you won't fit in there."

I hear her warning loud and clear, but it didn't really need saying. I've no intention of befriending the cheerleaders, that kind of thing's not really my scene. I'm much happier hiding behind my camera and slinking into the background.

Chelsea flounces off and I can't help my eyes from following her out toward *her* group. I can see from here that it consists of her squad and the football team. I can also see the longing in other student's eyes as they walk past them. They either want to be them or want to be part of their stupid little gang.

Jesus, this place is even more stereotypical than I was expecting.

Unfortunately, my first class of the day is in the direction Chelsea just went. I pull my bag up higher on my shoulder and hold the couple of books I have tighter to my chest as I walk out of the doors.

I've not taken two steps out of the building when my skin tingles with awareness. I tell myself to keep my head down. I've no interest in being their entertainment but my eyes defy me, and I find myself looking up as Chelsea points at me and laughs. I knew my sudden arrival in the town wasn't a secret. My mum's legacy is still strong, so when they heard the news, I'm sure it was hot gossip.

Heat spreads from my cheeks and down my neck. I go to look away when a pair of blue eyes catch my attention. While everyone else's look intrigued, like they've got a new pet to play with, his are haunted and angry. Our stare holds, his eyes narrow as if he's trying to warn me of something before he menacingly shakes his head.

Confused by his actions, I manage to rip my eyes from his and turn toward where I think I should be going.

I only manage three steps at the most before I crash into something—or somebody.

"Shit, I'm sorry. Are you okay?" a deep voice asks. When I look into the kind green eyes of the guy in front of me, I almost sigh with relief. I was starting to wonder if I'd find anyone who wasn't just going to glare at me. I know I'm the new girl but shit. They must experience new kids on a weekly basis, I can't be that unusual.

"I'm fine, thank you."

"You're the new British girl. Emily, right?"

"It's Amalie, and yeah... that's me."

"I'm so sorry about your parents. Mom said she was friends with yours." Tears burn my eyes. Today is hard enough without the constant reminder of everything I've lost. "Shit, I'm sorry. I shouldn't have—"

"It's fine," I lie.

"What's your first class?"

Handing over my timetable, he quickly runs his eyes over it. "English lit, I'm heading that way. Can I walk you?"

"Yes." His smile grows at my eagerness and for the first time today my returning one is almost sincere.

"I'm Shane, by the way." I look over and smile at him, thankfully the hallway is too noisy for us to continue any kind of conversation.

He seems like a sweet guy but my head's spinning and just the thought of trying to hold a serious conversation right now is exhausting.

Student's stares follow my every move. My skin prickles as more and more notice me as I walk beside Shane. Some give me smiles but most just nod in my direction, pointing me out to their friends. Some are just downright rude and physically point at me like I'm some fucking zoo animal awoken from its slumber.

In reality, I'm just an eighteen-year-old girl who's starting somewhere new, and desperate to blend into the crowd. I know that with who I am—or more who my parents were—that it's not going to be all that easy, but I'd at least like a chance to try to be normal. Although I fear I might have lost that the day I lost my parents.

"This is you." Shane's voice breaks through my thoughts and when I drag my head up from avoiding everyone else around me, I see he's holding the door open.

Thankfully the classroom's only half full, but still, every single set of eyes turn to me.

Ignoring their attention, I keep my head down and find an empty desk toward the back of the room.

Once I'm settled, I risk looking up. My breath catches when I find Shane still standing in the doorway, forcing the students entering to squeeze past him. He nods his head. I know it's his way of asking if I'm okay. Forcing a smile onto my lips, I nod in return and after a few seconds, he turns to leave.

THORN and the rest of the ROSEWOOD series are now LIVE.

DOWNLOAD TO CONTINUE READING